Right Here, Right Now

ALSO BY SHANNON DUNLAP

Izzy + Tristan

Right Here, Right Now

SHANNON DUNLAP

Little, Brown and Company
New York Boston

Copyright © 2024 by Shannon Dunlap
Atom image © Omeris/Shutterstock.com

Cover art copyright © 2024 by Jill De Haan. Cover design by Gabrielle Chang. Cover copyright © 2024 by Hachette Book Group, Inc.

Interior design by Gabrielle Chang.

Hachette Book Group
1290 Avenue of the Americas, New York, NY 10104
Visit us at LBYR.com

First Edition: April 2024

Little, Brown and Company is a division of Hachette Book Group, Inc. The Little, Brown name and logo are trademarks of Hachette Book Group, Inc.

The publisher is not responsible for websites (or their content) that are not owned by the publisher.

Little, Brown and Company books may be purchased in bulk for business, educational, or promotional use. For information, please contact your local bookseller or the Hachette Book Group Special Markets Department at special.markets@hbgusa.com.

Library of Congress Cataloging-in-Publication Data
Names: Dunlap, Shannon, author.
Title: Right here, right now / Shannon Dunlap.
Description: First edition. | New York : Little, Brown and Company, 2024. | Audience: Ages 14 and up. | Summary: Across alternate universes and varying scenarios, the paths of two musicians, Anna and Liam, consistently intertwine as they forge a connection.
Identifiers: LCCN 2023017460 | ISBN 9780316415422 (hardcover) | ISBN 9780316415439 (ebook)
Subjects: CYAC: Interpersonal relations—Fiction. | Space and time—Fiction. | Musicians—Fiction. | LCGFT: Novels.
Classification: LCC PZ7.1.D8637 Ri 2024 | DDC [Fic]—dc23
LC record available at https://lccn.loc.gov/2023017460

ISBNs: 978-0-316-41542-2 (hardcover), 978-0-316-41543-9 (ebook)

Printed in the United States of America

LSC-C

Printing 1, 2024

For the physicists, the artists,
and anyone else who tries to see
the universe in all its beautiful complexity

Overture

The enigma at the heart of quantum reality can be summed up in a single motto: what we see when we look at the world seems to be fundamentally different from what actually is.

—SEAN CARROLL, quantum physicist

1

AT ONE SINGLE POINT of time and space in a single world, Anna is making herself macaroni and cheese from a box. She is not, however, thinking about the macaroni, which is, at this very moment, cooking to a softness far south of appetizing. She is not even thinking about the topic she told herself she would think about during this short break, which is her solo piece for the audition. If it's all she thinks about for the few remaining days until the tryout, she still won't be able to perform it perfectly.

Instead, Anna is thinking about plunging her left hand into the pot of salt water that is boiling rapidly on the stove. She has this variety of thought frequently, though she would never really do it, obviously. It's sort of like standing near a high ledge and having the inexplicable impulse to jump. She has imagined slamming her wrist in a window, having it bitten completely off by Wendell, the noisy German shepherd next door, kneeling on the concrete of the driveway so that her parents' car can back its rear tire slowly over her metacarpals. Her hand and wrist throb constantly from so much practice, and she tells herself that these strange visions are simply her way of mentally coping with the pain, of owning it in some small way.

The abrupt ring of the phone echoes in the quiet house. Anna makes no move to answer it. Who calls in the middle of the afternoon, anyway? Only salespeople or some agency doing surveys. Or Elise. God, it's probably Elise. Anna closes her eyes, waits until it finishes ringing, then waits a few seconds more until it starts ringing again. Definitely Elise.

Elise has been her best friend since they took swimming lessons together when they were five years old. That's still how she would introduce her to someone—"This is my best friend, Elise"—but over the past few months the title has felt a little worn, like a sweater that's gotten too tight, and Anna has had a hard time feeling anything but annoyance for Elise. She is too much, too much of everything.

Anna wants only to be *something*—specifically, one of the greatest violinists the world has ever produced. Once upon a time, her mother had wanted her to follow in her footsteps, though the flaws in this plan became abundantly clear when four-year-old Anna wept through her first three dance recitals. When she picked up the violin in a school music class for the first time, it was like a weight inside her had suddenly become a balloon: Here was the thing that was going to make her special. But lately, Anna doesn't know how to catch up to that greatness or grasp it with her aching hand.

The sound of the phone dies, and then Anna realizes that she's forgotten to set the kitchen timer and curses under her breath. It's past time to drain the pasta, mix in the butter and the milk and the cheese powder and the frozen broccoli, and shovel it in before going back to practicing.

Usually her weird, violent daydreams fade quickly, but today they persist, nipping at the back of her brain the entire time she is standing at the counter and chewing the too-soft pasta and too-crunchy broccoli. Her wrist is a stick of dynamite, ready to blow into a million pieces of shrapnel. She tucks her left hand in her armpit like a broken wing while she eats with her right. What would her life be without it? If she didn't play the violin, would she even be the same person? She knows: technically, yes. And yet, it's hard to imagine a world in which she doesn't have music to anchor her life in place.

"Can we *please* focus?" Liam says. They've been in Gavin's parents' garage for almost two hours, and they've gotten through the new song a shockingly small number of times. Gavin is trying to hold them all together on drums, but Chris's guitar solo is so heavy and plodding that it sounds like he's dragging a dead body around, and Eric's bass line is halting and unsteady, as if he unwittingly tripped on that same corpse and lost his balance. There's a headache developing behind Liam's right eye. He feels in his gut that "Dark Dark Matter" is good or could be, but Chris and Eric cannot bring it to life. No matter how much electrical jolt he pours into the vocals, all he gets back is a flatline.

"The show is in less than two weeks," he reminds them.

"Is the show in less than two weeks?" Eric asks, mock-innocent. "Really? You haven't mentioned that eight thousand times." Desperate for productivity, Liam has made an authoritarian decree, forbidding any kind of smoking or drinking during this rehearsal, but this dictatorial move has backfired, making Eric irritable and causing Chris to gripe under his breath about lead singers everywhere who think they're the center of the universe.

Chris snickers at Eric's comment, and Liam feels like punching Chris in the face. He doesn't even like Chris, but it's impossible to find a decent lead guitar in this town. He wishes he could get someone like his cousin Elise to learn to play; she would have a million times more stage presence than Chris, even if she has no discernible musical talent.

"If you guys ever played like you were real musicians, maybe I'd keep my mouth shut," Liam mutters.

Gavin raises an eyebrow at Liam, then calmly sets his drumsticks down on a nearby stack of paint cans and folds his arms, waiting for the inevitable argument to play out. Gavin has a nature boy/Buddhist monk thing going on, which would be annoying in its own way if it weren't so damn genuine.

"In what world does you acting like an asshole make us a better band, Liam?" Chris says, his voice taking on that pious and wronged tone that drives Liam insane.

They start engaging in the same old fight; Liam could wage his side of the battle in his sleep by now. His eye continues to throb, and Chris's phrase "in what world" keeps repeating in his head, jangling something uneasily inside him. He thinks fairly often, actually, of the Many-Worlds concept that Ms. Keeley taught them last year in physics, that quantum mechanics mind-bender in which the universe keeps on branching into copies of itself, over and over again. There's a version of the universe in which Chris isn't such a prick, another in which Eric isn't such a disappointment. There's a version of the universe in which he, Liam, is already recognized by the world as a musical genius. There's a version of the universe in which Julian is still alive, in which the very marrow of Liam turned out to be enough to save him. But that's not the version he's living in.

The air-conditioning in the aging hatchback is crap, so Elise has the window rolled down all the way, her left forearm propped up to catch the breeze. It's one of those last sweaty days of August, the humidity and the coming school year bearing down in equal measure. She hasn't been driving long; she only got her license at the beginning of summer. And yet, she knows this stretch of road well, near the midpoint on the route to her job at the mall, where she piles slices of meat and cheese, soggy pickles, and a confetti of iceberg lettuce onto sandwich buns for the masses of harried shoppers and exercising grannies and bored teenagers who parade through the food court every day. She's running late, only slightly, but there's a big slow-moving pickup truck in front of her: Pale blue, starting to rust in patches, it has a bumper sticker on the back that says MY KID BEAT UP YOUR HONOR STUDENT. She swings her car out into the left lane.

Maybe she does it because she can already envision the annoyed look on her coworker Kent's face when she shows up past the time she's supposed to relieve him. Kent is boring— all he talks about is basketball practice and his stupid girl-friend, Andrea—but even so, she would rather not listen to him complain as soon as she arrives.

Maybe she does it because she is the type of person who always chooses action over inaction, who sees a situation, any situation, and immediately feels the itch to change it.

Or maybe she does it out of some darker, deeply buried impulse, some desire to stand on a high ledge and feel the urge to jump.

It doesn't matter. The universe branches because of particles almost too tiny to imagine, not because of human choice.

Both vehicles are descending a slight hill, and when Elise accelerates to pass the pickup, the truck picks up speed, too. The problem is that there is a garbage truck approaching them rapidly from the opposite direction. Her brain is a panicky firework of indecision, and she doesn't know whether to slow down or speed up.

She guns the engine to get past the pickup.

On the radio, the singer warbles that she is torn.

What is Elise thinking about in that moment, the moment when the menacing face of the truck is rushing toward her? Not her cousin, who is smoking a joint with the drummer of his band twenty miles away in an abandoned woodshed and trying to forget the frustrations of the day's practice. Not her childhood friend, who is sitting on the edge of her yellow bedspread, trying to shake the ache out of her left hand before playing her solo selection for the upcoming orchestra audition again and again and again. And not, certainly, the quantum physicist Hugh Everett or his Many Worlds, because Elise has never heard of him and doesn't have as ambitious of a high school physics teacher as her cousin. She thinks, instead, about a memory from a long time ago, when she was jumping on a neighbor's trampoline, jumping and jumping until the sensation of her stomach jouncing up and down became acutely uncomfortable and yet she could not bring herself to stop, and even when she did stop, there was still part of her jumping, a shadow self that could not be still.

In 1954, Hugh Everett tried to understand how electrons could really be part of a wave function, existing in more than one place at a time. His insight was that not only are the particles in multiple locations at once, but so are we, the observers. Humans ride the wave function of the universe in exactly the same way that tiny particles do. Elise shoots toward the garbage truck and an electron shoots through space; the electron spins not right *or* left, but both. Right *and* left. The world splits into two branches, one more duplication in a near-infinite array of possibilities.

The electron spins to the left, and in one world, Elise's car pulls ahead, the drivers of both trucks hit their brakes, and she easily slides back into the right lane. The only ripple of what has happened is in the irritated bleat of the garbage truck's horn and in the racing of her heart for a few seconds until the song on the radio changes and the pickup recedes slightly behind her and the moment gets swallowed by the normalcy of a late-summer afternoon. Of course it does.

Except that in another branch of the multiverse, it doesn't.

2

THE ELECTRON SPINS TO THE RIGHT.

I ALREADY KNOW THAT I'm preaching to the choir, but I let the rant spill out of me anyway: "It's what sets us apart. Why would we want to water down our sound into bullshit mainstream radio gruel? If anything, we should get harder, faster."

I stop talking and close my eyes against the angry blur of my own words, trying to let a disorienting moment pass. This happens sometimes, this feeling that I am so small that I spin wildly in circles like a tiny subatomic particle without the power to affect anything. A ghost particle. It helps to remind myself: I am Liam, I am a real person, the world really exists, and so does our band.

When I open my eyes, Gavin is slowly picking apart a twig into a pile of curly splinters, a perfect little fire starter if he were setting up camp. Practice long over, we're sitting in the woods behind his house, his natural habitat. He made Eagle Scout the year before, though no one who sees him dressed in his starched Scout uniform would ever guess that he's a pretty badass metal drummer in his spare time.

"Yeah," Gavin says. "But Chris just wants to pretend he's Stevie Ray Vaughan or something. And Eric...who knows? He wants to play whatever kind of music will get him the most drugs." He laughs. Gavin is always willing to listen to me vent, but he never gets as upset about this stuff as I do, which sometimes makes talking to him worse than not complaining to anyone at all.

I can feel every little muscle in my arms when I stand up to stretch; I'm still sort of stoned. At least the headache is gone. It would be so easy to stay here and let time wash out from under me, but I need to get home. My ability to avoid my father has been particularly on point lately, but it requires keeping to a strict schedule. I offer my hand to Gavin for a farewell handshake, and he pulls me toward him for a brief manly hug. He's my only friend who would do such a thing, and I'd never tell him how much I like it, how much I admire how easy and natural everything seems for him.

The wooded slope down to the car is muddy, and even though there's no one to see, I'm vaguely embarrassed by my constant small slips and missteps, and my boots that are clearly constructed for looks and not functionality. Gavin's family owns a bunch of land way out here in the sticks, and usually I look forward to the peaceful drive back to town— the full summer trees, the deer eating in the fields that line the road—but tonight I'm too distracted by Chris and Eric and all their bullshit. I want to sing songs that will make people's heads explode; why is that not a goal of literally everyone on the planet? And yet, no one seems to get it. Muriel had come the closest, I guess, even if she wasn't a musician, but the whole time we were together, Muriel was caught up in her own cyclone of problems.

As the world blurs beyond the side windows, I envision that I'm being carried down the road by a sound wave racing its way around the globe. It scoops up those who understand the meaning of rock and sucks the rest down into its current.

I was nine years old when I heard "Smells Like Teen Spirit" for the first time, and I was shocked that Earth hadn't been knocked off its axis, sent spinning end over end by the crashing, cataclysmic sound. But that was a long time ago, and now it is 1998, the radio waves themselves practically yawning every time a new Nickelback or Creed song cycles blandly through them, and it is way past time for the great What's Next. It is the dawn of a new millennium of music, and I know that I'm supposed to be part of it. If only Eric and Chris would really try once in a while. If only I knew how to show the world how great we could be.

I'm still deep into the puzzle of the newest song when I

walk into the kitchen. I know instantly that something is way off. There's a charge to the air, that sick static of life going off the rails. It's also quiet—no television, no radio, no sounds of Mom and Dad conversing or making dinner—and bad things always happen in silence.

Mom is sitting at the counter alone, her eyes rimmed in red as if she's been crying, a glass of white wine half empty in front of her. When she speaks, her voice is hoarse and on the verge of breaking.

"It's Elise," she says. "There's been an accident."

3

THE ELECTRON SPINS TO THE LEFT.

"IT'S ELISE," SHE SAYS.

I've been standing here with the bow quiet on the strings, imagining myself floating in space, convincing myself that I am Anna, that I am a famous musician in the making, that I can nail this audition, that I am a massive and unstoppable planetary force, when my mother's voice breaks my reverie. "It's Elise," she says again. I open my eyes and shake my head like a dog with an ear problem, hoping she'll take the hint, but she only shrugs and lets the bedroom door swing open a little wider and retreats down the hallway.

Elise sweeps in with the dramatic air of a Hollywood starlet and flops immediately on my bed, ignoring that I'm in the middle of visualizing the slender margin of perfection necessary for this piece. It is nearly impossible, one of Paganini's

"24 Caprices," which even my violin teacher, Mr. Foster, who is nothing if not arrogant, has tried to talk me out of playing.

Elise is still wearing her pale blue Submarine Dreams work polo, a small blob of dried mustard staining her left shoulder.

"Two hours of work before they sent me home. Can you believe that? It's like *barely* enough to cover gas."

"Elise, I have to practice. I'm super stressed about this audition. I told you that yesterday." It's not a lie; I have my last pre-audition private lesson tomorrow, and as much as I dislike my time with Mr. Foster, he's so irritatingly talented (and his rates so expensive, as my father is always grumbling) that I have to make my time with him worth it. I cradle the violin like a ukulele, strum the strings so softly that they make no sound. This is a dance that Elise and I have done before, so I'm ready for it. Setting the violin down in its case right now will only lengthen the time before I manage to convince Elise to leave, so I keep it out and engaged, like a weapon.

Elise pushes herself up on her elbows and sighs. "Yes, the audition. The axis around which our days must turn."

"*Your* days don't have to turn around it, just mine," I tell her. "Weren't you complaining last week that they overscheduled you? And that you hated your coworkers? Now you have free time."

"Well, gee whiz, Pollyanna, thanks for sorting all my problems." Elise wrinkles her nose. It's unfair that she's still so much cuter than me, even when she's making such an ugly face.

Once, when I was a toddler, I fell out the window of the second-story apartment we were living in at the time, and to the amazement of the emergency room physicians, I emerged from the incident completely unscathed. "So lucky," my father always says about the fall, but my mother takes a more metaphysical view, as she does about most things. She describes seeing me alive and well in the hospital like it was a religious experience. "You smiled at me, just like when you were a tiny baby. It was like you'd been born a second time," she always says. "That's how I knew you'd be twice as great as anything we'd imagined."

Sometimes I look at Elise, at her brightness and energy and effortless creativity, at her general ease with being herself, at how things always seem to go her way, and I think that maybe the universe mixed us up somehow. She's the special one, the one kissed by destiny. I'm just...me. Just Anna, a plodding workhorse, tricked by my mother's silly story into chasing something impossible.

"Can we *please* go out and do something?" Elise asks. She absentmindedly picks up a Greenville High T-shirt that's lying on the bed and scrubs at the mustard stain with it. It's nothing, really; it's only a shirt that I use to sleep in anyway, but I can feel the claws of irritation flexing themselves in my chest.

There is, of course, a part of me that wants to say yes, that wants to forget everything and go hang out with Elise, but that part is weak and puny and crushed under the gravity of greater responsibilities. The only real option in situations like this is to ignore Elise altogether and go on playing, which is surely the fastest method of making her leave since she has no appreciation for violin and never has. She once called the violin "guitar for boring people."

Instead of playing the solo piece, however, I dabble in a short bit of Fanny Mendelssohn's "Overture in C," one of those fragments that sometimes gets stuck in my head. Poor old Fanny—ragged on by her family, who ignored her talent and just wanted to marry her off, always in the musical shadow of her stupid brother Felix. Fanny was a striver, too, for all the good it did her.

Elise sighs and hauls herself off the bed as if the music itself, this one thing that keeps me afloat as a human being, is a heavy burden that rests constantly on her shoulders. I don't quite catch what she says before she walks out the door, but it's something like, "Have fun being the loneliest person in the world."

1

Every quantum transition taking place on every star, in every galaxy, in every remote corner of the universe is splitting our local world on earth into myriads of copies of itself.

—BRYCE DeWITT, quantum physicist

4

TO THE RIGHT

JESUS, I'VE NEVER BEEN to a wake before. That doesn't make a bit of sense, but it's true nonetheless, and the full weirdness of the fact hits me while I'm standing there in the same room as Elise's coffin. Everyone else here seems to know what to do; they speak quietly, smile sadly, put their arms around Aunt Caroline's shoulders, stand for a long time in front of the table that holds framed photos of Elise. It all seems choreographed and tremendously fake, and it makes me want to do something to explode the scene: tear my hair out or smash one of the picture frames on the floor or scream the final note of the song I was writing last night, tentatively titled "Bathtub of Blood."

But then, there's my father, staring daggers at me. If anyone fits in here, it's him, painted as he always is in a spectrum of grays. He tenses his lower jaw one degree more and looks as though he can read my mind. If I were to really follow any of my fleeting destructive impulses, it would enrage him, and it wouldn't matter if I explained to him that Elise wouldn't have minded in the slightest. Elise and I coexisted through all family functions with zero friction. She was cute and zany, two qualities that I don't usually seek out in a companion, but Elise also had a rebel spirit that I had to respect. And then, shockingly, she'd gone and run her car head-on into a giant garbage truck, which was totally fucking psycho and the most breathtakingly death metal thing imaginable.

A woman with carefully arranged hair and a yellow sweater set appears soundlessly at my elbow and touches my arm lightly.

"Water?" she says, and it sounds like a code word until I notice that she is offering me a bottle of water.

"Me?" I say dumbly, but I take the bottle out of her hand.

"You're the brother, aren't you? I'm so sorry for your loss," she says with a practiced sympathy and a tilt of her head.

At the word *brother*, my stomach does a backflip, as if this random funeral parlor employee can see deep inside me to the locked box where I keep anything related to Julian. But she can't, obviously. This is Elise's funeral, and she's mistaking me for my cousin David. "I ... I'm just a cousin," I stammer.

"Oh," she says, "well." Then she departs again to drift silently through the crowd, prepared to hydrate more serious mourners. I should have said something else, I guess. Now I am left with a bottle of water that I don't want or know what to do with, so I sip at it awkwardly and then chug half of it to get rid of it more quickly. Dad looks over at me again and mouths the words *Stop that*, and when I look down at my hands, I see that I've been squeezing and releasing the flimsy sides of the bottle, producing an annoying sound without even noticing. I decide to walk around a little.

I avoid the side of the room that holds the coffin. It's closed now, thankfully, but earlier, when it was only family here, we'd had a few minutes when we could enter the room before they lowered the lid on the casket. I waited in the hallway. It came over me like a wave, the fear that I might pass out or get sick if I looked at dead Elise. When I balked at the idea, my father's lip had curled into a sneer of derision. This at least made sense, because it was similar to how I felt about myself in that moment; I was the person who had written the song "Corpse Lover," the person who had delivered the "Poor Yorick" monologue in my high school production of *Hamlet*, and then I couldn't bring myself to be in the same room as a dead body. Mom awkwardly rubbed my back and said that I should do whatever I felt was best, though I should consider that seeing Elise might "give me a little bit of closure." Huh? She'd never given me the option to have any closure over Julian, but before I could think of what to say to her, she'd slipped inside the room to be with her sister, and I was left standing, trying not to make eye contact with the dark-suited men who hurried past looking for the restroom. *We fat ourselves for maggots.* Shakespeare would totally be a heavy metal singer if he were alive today.

Anyway, the coffin is safely closed now, but that section of the room still seems like a suckhole of sadness. I feel better in the outer orbits of the crowd, which is filled with people who don't want to be here almost as much as I don't want to be here. There is a cluster of middle-aged people who occasionally talk or wave to the teenagers in the room, and it's clear that these are the teachers from Elise's school. Some of them look genuinely broken up, the skin around their eyes all pink and puffy, while others look merely antsy and ready to flee.

"Liam, isn't it?" one of them says. It's a man wearing an embarrassingly threadbare cardigan sweater, and I don't know him, but I know he's a choir teacher even before he outs himself as such. "I saw you perform at the regional choral competition last spring. Very impressive solo."

"Um, thanks," I murmur. It's not that I don't like compliments, but I really don't feel like taking center stage right now, and this man has an attention-grabbing bullhorn of a voice, which is often the case with people who spend their days talking to people about breath control. Some of Elise's classmates eye us curiously.

"What groups will you be performing with next year?" the man asks.

"I'm not sure." The truth is that I plan to give up on choir this year, because I'm sick of people like this guy, just the same sad people year after year, acting like I'm letting them down if I don't feel like singing Bach's "Honor and Glory" for the millionth time. I've been avoiding making this news public, though, since my mom will be disappointed and my dad will act, once again, like all his suspicions about my character have been confirmed. I mumble something polite and nonsensical to the nosy choir guy and edge toward a corner of the room where I saw a trash can earlier. I'd like to ditch this water bottle, at least.

In front of the trash can, some high school kids are listening to a guy in a varsity jacket talk about Elise.

"When she didn't show up on time, it's like I just *knew*, you know? It's like that—you just know. How? I don't know. It's like goose bumps on your nutsack or something." An impossibly pale girl leans her head on his shoulder as if he's said something very deep or even true.

I told myself on the car ride over that I was not going to be a dick to Elise's friends because it wouldn't be the first time I came off as such. (Don't ask me why; I'm usually thinking about song lyrics or something, not the playbook of how to be an asshole, but enough people have told me I am one that I've come to accept it as at least partially true.) Elise was always cool not only to me but also to any of my friends she happened to meet. She once told Gavin that he probably would have been the first explorer to reach the South Pole if he'd only been born a little earlier, and I think it's the only time I've ever seen him blush. So I should strive for reciprocity here. But really, who is this varsity jacket guy? Most people in the circle are smiling or nodding at him, but one girl in a navy-blue dress with her arms folded over her chest gives an undisguised eye roll. This is all the encouragement I need to check the guy roughly with my shoulder on the way to the trash can.

"Whoa," Varsity Jacket says. "Watch it."

"Fuck off." The hard slam of my shoulder into his has made my spirit lift in a way that all the bottled water in the world could never manage.

"You starting something with me at a funeral, bro?" Varsity Jacket says. His eyes glance sideways, and I get that he's being held in check because a bunch of his teachers are a few paces away. But I don't care who's here, and I'd love an excuse to punch someone right now.

"It's a wake, not a funeral," I tell him. "And stop talking about my dead cousin's effect on your nutsack." Out of the corner of my eye, I see the girl in the blue dress turn and walk away. I wish I could have seen the expression on her face when she did, to know if she was pleased or exasperated.

Varsity Jacket puts his hands up in a conciliatory way. Then I hear, "Liam?" right behind me and realize my mom has walked up without me knowing it, and now these supposed friends of Elise are cowering in her presence. Give me a break. Here they are, near-adults, but they cringe and act like little children whenever a parent appears. I am always myself, at least.

"Sorry to interrupt," Mom says, with an acid glance at Varsity Jacket, and my heart briefly blooms with love for her. No matter what else goes on between us, I appreciate that she has good instincts about who to trust and has always been able to smell bullshit from a mile away. "Liam, can you help me get a few things from the car?"

I nod and follow her, ignoring the cloud of whispers we leave behind. We walk in silence out of the room and through the somber marble lobby of the funeral home, and out to where my father's SUV is parked behind the building, and then she exhales loudly and says, "Now. I need one of those cigarettes that I know you have."

This is an eyebrow raiser. "You don't smoke."

"I do today."

"Fair enough." I dig a crumpled pack of American Spirits from where they've been hibernating deep in my jacket pocket, shake out two, and search for a lighter. My mom leans against the car while she waits and crosses her ankles, turning her face up to the sun.

I've always known that she is pretty, but seeing her like this, the cigarette dangling from her fingers, it makes my chest go tight with renewed admiration. She's older than most of my friends' moms—there was a seven-year gap between me and Julian—but she's classier, too. The way she leans into the flame when I offer it, dressed all in black, looks like something out of an old French movie.

"These will hurt your voice, you know," she says, after a few moments of quiet smoking.

"I know. That's why I don't do it much. Hardly ever. I only keep them in case some degenerate tries to bum one in a parking lot."

She doesn't crack a smile. "Why are you starting fights at your cousin's funeral?"

"It's not a funeral. It's a wake."

"I can't handle you and your father fighting with each other. Not today."

Of course, this is really about Dad. I should have guessed from her gray expression. "He doesn't need to make everything I do about himself. Why does it matter what shoes I'm wearing?" This is a reference to an earlier fight in which my loving father had demanded that I change clothes before he allowed me into the car, and Mom had brokered an uneasy peace by saying that I could wear my favorite jeans and what she referred to as "that somewhat tired jacket" if I traded my combat boots for a pair of my father's dress shoes.

My mother puts up her hands to stop the flow of words. "Not today, Liam," she repeats.

I shrug. Whatever. I'll just avoid him for a couple days

if that's what will make her happy. I kick the toe of his shoe against the dusty tire.

"The whole family is here, and I keep thinking Elise is about to show up," I say. "And then I remember. It sucks."

"Yes. It does. It certainly sucks."

"How's Aunt Caroline holding up?"

"Not well, but that's to be expected," Mom says, taking a deep drag on the cigarette and then stooping to tap it out on the asphalt. "God, I can't believe this happened to both of us. She makes me crazy, but she was so, so good to me after Julian died. She was the only thing that got me through those first weeks." She shoots me an uneasy glance after she says this.

"It's okay," I tell her. "I was five. Not exactly an emotional rock."

"Well, the fact of your existence was a rock, at least, if not our day-to-day interactions." She sighs. "Anyway, I keep trying to remember all the things Caroline said and did so I can do the same for her, but it's like going back there, you know? After spending all this time trying not to think about it. It's exhausting."

I'm not sure what to say to this, so I nod. It's not as if I actually believe her when she says that my existence mattered back then. I puzzle for a moment over whether or not she has truly convinced herself that this was the case.

"I'm talking too much," she says. She holds out her

cigarette and I take it from her. "I need to get back in there. Throw these away before they give you cancer." I can tell that she means this as a joke, then realizes what she's said, and tears well up in her eyes. She shakes her head. "Forget I said that."

"It's okay, Mom," I say, even though my chest feels like someone is tightening an iron band around it. She never mentions anything that is even tangentially related to Julian. "It's just a bad day."

She clears her throat, getting her game face back on. "You can say that again. Don't pick fights with your father. Or strangers." She points her finger at me and looks on the verge of saying something else, but instead, she turns on her heel and walks back toward the building.

It's boiling hot, and I'm still wearing my jacket. I can tell that I have big sweat rings going, so I move to the patch of shade on the other side of the car, even though I already know it's not going to help. I drop both cigarettes, barely smoked, onto the asphalt and flatten them with my toe. There's a little wooded area behind the funeral home and the cicadas are making a racket. It would be almost peaceful if the circumstances were even slightly different.

That's when I notice the girl in the blue dress sitting in the driver's seat of a car a few yards away. Her eyes are closed. I almost laugh because this is a really weird place for a nap, but a few seconds later, she's still entirely motionless, more frozen than sleep. My heart speeds up. What if there's something wrong with her? Is that a thing that happens, people having heart attacks or strokes or something from a rush of grief?

I walk over, slowly, ready to turn back if she moves before I reach her, but she doesn't. When I knock on her window, she doesn't jerk back to alertness as if she's been startled awake. She simply blinks her eyes open and stares at me, as if she's been expecting a visitor. The effect is eerie and alluring all rolled into one, and I can't tell if I've landed in the middle of a horror film or a remake of *Sleeping Beauty*. For a second, I feel like running away, but she's already rolling down the window.

"Yes?" she asks matter-of-factly. Violin music flows from the car's stereo, the notes climbing higher and higher.

"I'm Liam," I say.

"I know who you are," she says, reaching over to turn off the music. She does it with a sharp little turn of her wrist, cutting the notes off so abruptly it's almost like she's snapping something in two. Did I do something to offend this girl?

"Oh," I say. "Because of what I said to that guy in there? If he's a friend of yours, I apologize."

"Kent McHenry is a world-class asshole," she says flatly, and I recognize that she's not so much angry as trying to keep all emotions at bay. It's a strategy I'm deeply familiar with. Anyway, she's cool enough not to buy what Varsity Jacket is selling, so I decide not to run away after all. She looks up at me, using her hand to shade her eyes from the sun. "That's not how I know who you are. I used to see you at Elise's house all the time. When we were little kids."

Some memories gain shape and begin to surface. There was a span of—what? A few months? An entire year?—when I was too young to stay by myself after school while my parents were both at work. Aunt Caroline used to pick me up, because back then I was in the same school district as her kids, even though Elise and I went to different elementary schools. And yeah, there had often been another girl running around in the backyard with Elise, making up strange dance routines and clambering around on a tire swing. I never paid much attention to them, because even though they were only a year younger, they seemed babyish, though now I can't remember why exactly. And then everything shifted at some point—we'd moved to our current house, which was in the Mercer school district, and my mom had switched to being a realtor and had more flexible hours, and I'd had my own stuff to do after school anyway.

"Sure," I say. "I remember now."

"You don't," she says. "But it's okay."

"Sorry. It's been a long time." It's late afternoon by now, but the sun is hot on my back, and I wipe the sweat from my neck. I should take off the jacket, but then my dad's stupid shoes will look even worse. "Remind me of your name?"

"Anna," she says, sticking her hand out the window as if it's a formal introduction, and I take it in mine. Hands are not, as a rule, something I notice about someone, but hers is beautiful—slender and smooth and slightly cool to the touch. It's like a sculpture of a hand. Then she puts both hands on the steering wheel and sighs and stares out the windshield. "I don't want to go back in there. At least, not until there are fewer people. If one more person tells me that at least I have my memories of her, I will scream. Like not hypothetically. I will actually scream."

I, too, should go back inside, play nice, think sad thoughts about Elise. But my dad can't get mad at me if I'm not even there, can he?

"Do you want to go somewhere else?" I ask. "For a little while?"

She keeps her eyes trained forward like she hasn't heard me, but I can tell she's considering it, and then she looks at me and nods. "Yeah, why not?" she says. "Get in."

5

TO THE LEFT

"SO WHEN DO YOU find out?" Elise asks.

There's a petulant edge to her voice that sort of makes me want to hang up on her, except that I would never do something so rude. Elise has definitely hung up on me before, but Elise can get away with all kinds of things that I would never attempt. I haven't seen her since she left my bedroom in a huff, even though the audition was two days ago.

"Probably in the next few days," I say. I prop the cordless phone under my chin so I can rub my left wrist. The dark visions of maiming myself have subsided since the audition, but the ache in my wrist hasn't. "What do you have planned this weekend? I could use something to take my mind off the wait."

"I don't know if you'd be interested," Elise says.

Honestly, sometimes talking to Elise is like cajoling a three-year-old. I try to inject some genuine enthusiasm into my voice before I say, "Try me."

"You know my cousin Liam?" Elise asks, and my heart adds a little grace note before the next beat.

Liam. Of course I know Liam. It's not just that Elise brings him up from time to time, the way someone does with a favorite cousin. It's that I had a big fat crush on him as a child and spent hours at Elise's house distracted from whatever Elise and I were doing while I secretly schemed over how to win him over. He'd had the most arresting long eyelashes, and even as a kid he was moody and mysterious and confident in his own opinions, and all of it convinced me he was the most interesting human being on earth.

There was one afternoon when Elise and I talked Liam into recording a radio show with us on an old cassette recorder that had belonged to Elise's father. We spent hours on the script: Elise was the DJ, Liam performed all the music, pretending to be a different act with every song, and I was assigned to sound effects, ripping up paper and shaking things in a box on cue. When I layered several tracks of music on Elise's keyboard for one of his songs, he was obviously impressed.

"How'd you learn to do that?" he'd asked.

"Natural talent," I'd said. "And Suzuki piano lessons when I was five."

He'd laughed then, and I'd floated on air for hours. The show was cut short because Liam's mom had come to pick him up, and by then he and Elise were arguing about whether or not to include a segment about the Shadow. (She was all for it; he was confused about why our show was suddenly set in the 1930s.) When I tried to interest them in completing it the next day, Liam was sullen about something and playing a game on the computer in the den. I ejected the tape before I left that day and hid it up my sleeve, secreting it home to listen to later, though now I can't remember if I ever did listen to it or where I hid it. It has to be around here; I wouldn't have thrown it away, because I certainly haven't forgotten the torch I carried for Liam, even if I'd rather die than admit that to Elise.

"You can say if you don't want to go," Elise is saying. "You don't have to sit there in silence thinking of an excuse."

"Hmm?" I say, snapping back to attention. "Sorry, the connection was bad for a few seconds there. I missed what you were saying."

"I *said* that Liam's band has a show at that pizza place near the railroad tracks this Saturday."

"That place that usually has the old guys in the Hawaiian shirts play on the weekends? Like a Jimmy Buffett cover band?" I am only half paying attention to the conversation, because I'm also dragging a chair over so I can climb up and reach the high shelf in the closet where I keep a box full of childhood treasures.

Elise sighs. "I don't know. Maybe? His band is metal, like very heavy metal. They're called Feral Soul. Or Fatal Soul, maybe? They've changed the name a few times." She pauses. "It might be horrible."

"No, it sounds fun," I say. I put the box on the bed and sift through the detritus of friendship bracelets and old birthday cards and little stuffed animals.

"Really?" Elise says.

I close my eyes, refocusing on patching things up with Elise. "I know I've been a drag lately." Honestly, I don't want to go. The band sounds ridiculous, and I don't want to tarnish the golden image of Liam I've kept for as long as the stuff in this box. But I also don't want Elise to be mad at me anymore. I want to glide through these last few days of summer, phone it in during my last few shifts at the ice cream shop, feel as carefree as everyone else seems to feel. And besides, there's always the chance that Liam will see me and immediately recognize the natural beauty and talent that is invisible to everyone else and then we will flee this mundane existence together and live a life of glamour and wild passion. Obviously. "I want to go."

"Let's go, then!" Elise says. She always forgives easily at the slightest suggestion of an apology. It's one of the things I love about her. "I'll pick you up in the Monopoly mobile at seven. We can eat before the show."

"Okay," I say, and I let Elise's excitement seep into me a little.

After I hang up, I look in the box again and my eyes go right to it—an audiocassette case with "ELA Productions" written on the paper insert in green Sharpie. Our initials, in what must be Liam's handwriting. I almost pick up the phone again to tell Elise about my discovery, but I don't. Elise's car, so old and tiny that it looks like you could use it as a Monopoly playing piece, has a tape deck, but I'm not sure I want to listen to this with Elise. I put the lid back on the box and heave the whole thing onto the shelf to continue collecting dust.

On Saturday, I put on my dark blue dress, a sweater, and a pair of cat's-eye earrings from my grandmother that come close to matching my eyes. I've checked the mailbox approximately eight million times today, waiting for an acceptance letter from the orchestra's conductor, Mr. Halloway. Nothing yet, though every time I open the little mailbox door, my stomach twists and then unclenches, releasing an ooze of disappointment. It's exhausting, and I wish I hadn't told Elise that I would go to the show with her. I just want this one thing to be certain, settled, even if it's bad news, but instead there's only endless limbo.

I stare into the bathroom mirror, put my hair in a pony-tail, take it out again, make an ugly face at myself, all the time wondering if Liam will remember who I am. I can hear Elise walk in the front door as if it's her own house and start talking to my mom.

"Whoa, sexy," Elise says when I give up on my hair and walk into the kitchen. I immediately wish I could retreat to my room and change. Elise is wearing tight dark jeans, high-heeled boots, and what looks like a band T-shirt with the neckline ripped out. Her short hair is mussed into spiky clumps, and it looks amazing, as usual. Elise is a chameleon who resists easy categorization. It's why most people at school don't know what to do with her; it's why I find her totally maddening but can't stop wondering what she might do next. Earlier in the day she might have been wearing an oversized flannel shirt or a string of pearls. She might have been instant messaging a pen pal in South Korea or painting a still life that looks like it came from a different age entirely. With Elise, anything is a possibility.

My mom looks up from where she's reading the newspaper at the kitchen counter, takes in the two of us. I wonder if it ever pains her to notice that her only daughter is almost always the least cool person in the room. My mother is a former dancer; the easy confidence of it still shows in every one of her molecules. Even now, in her loose-fitting shirt and leggings, my mom is probably dressed more appropriately for a concert than I am.

"Look at you two," she says. "You'll be careful on the roads, right?"

"Of course, Mrs. H," Elise says before I have a chance to respond. "What are you and the mister up to tonight?"

"Well," she says, laughing a little. "We've been taking ballroom lessons on Saturdays." Not long after my parents first met, years before I was born, a bad knee injury ended my mother's career early. The fact that my research-librarian father debases himself every week by schlepping around the dance floor next to his graceful wife can only be taken as a sign of true devotion. Everyone knows that his every decision, perhaps even the one that resulted in my existence, is designed only to make my mother happy. It's always seemed sort of silly, my father's puppy love, and yet...it would be hard to be upset if someone treated me the same way.

"Sounds hot," Elise says to my mom, and while the two of them giggle together, I have a few moments in which to search my purse for my lip gloss, resist the urge to ask my mother about the mail again, and ponder whether I was born into the wrong family somehow. Maybe I fell to Earth as a changeling all those years ago and the real Anna is dancing her heart out in some other realm.

"Be home by midnight," my mom says as we walk out the door, even though I'm pretty sure my parents won't be home to know if I'm back on time or not.

The pizza place is called Mozzarella on the Tracks, and I have always hated it: the preening, shirtless men playing volleyball on the court out back, the stupid punny names of the items on the menu (Mushroom with a View, Hamburger Waves of Grain), the ugly shorts on the families playing miniature golf at the place next door. I almost mention this last quibble aloud to Elise, but I bite my tongue. Elise is always quick to make my opinions seem petty and mean, even when they are only astute observations.

The cover band, the Lost Shakers, is loading out their gear from the earlier set when Elise and I put in our order for a medium Pizza My Heart. Elise flirts with the college-aged waiter, attempts to order a pitcher of beer despite the giant Xs on our hands that mark us as underage, then pretends to have been joking the whole time when he refuses. I feign deep interest in the menu, embarrassed.

"Hey, there's Liam," Elise says, and I twist around in my seat to watch him plugging cords into an amp. He looks mostly as I remember, though his shoulders are broader, his jaw a little sharper. He's dressed very simply in jeans and a black T-shirt, but his fingernails are painted black and he's wearing some sort of complicated bracelet that looks like it's made of medieval chain mail. He looks great, basically, and I hope that Elise doesn't notice the flush that I can feel climbing my neck.

"LEE. UM. LEE. UM," Elise chants in a deafening voice while I am still spying on him. "We're here! Anna thinks you look hot!"

I swing back around in my chair, but not before I see Liam

wave at her, obviously pleased. Elise waves back until I give her a kick under the table.

"Why do you always have to do stuff like that?" I hiss. "It's like you live to humiliate me."

Elise seems completely bewildered. The pizza lands on our table, and she stabs one of the artichoke hearts with her fork without bothering to move a slice to her plate. "Why would that embarrass you? Because you actually do think he's hot? Lots of people do. Like most people who aren't related to him by blood, I'm pretty sure."

"That's not the point," I say, flustered. I scowl and shake the crushed red pepper flakes that I know Elise hates all over my half of the pie so that she won't try to steal any of it.

"Actually, Anna thinks you look like shit!" Elise yells toward the stage. "But I think your bassist is cute." I steal the briefest of glances toward the band and see Liam exchanging grins with a rail-thin, shaggy blond kid, a baby-kitten version of Kurt Cobain. I sink low in my chair, cover my face with one forearm.

"Please stop," I say.

"Oh, come on, Anna. No one spends as much time thinking about you as you assume they do." There's a little venom in Elise's tone now as we edge closer to arguments we've had a million times before. I want to snap at her that people spend more time thinking she's an idiot than she assumes they do, but this is supposed to be a conciliatory evening, so instead, I take a giant bite of pizza and let the cheese scald the top of my mouth. So I'll never speak to Liam. I'll die miserable and alone. Whatever. That bracelet is weird anyway.

"Let's play Casting Director," I say, dredging up an old pastime of ours in a desperate attempt to change the subject. "The bassist is definitely Kurt Cobain."

"Not an actor and also dead, but okay, I see where you're coming from," Elise says. "Lead singer of the Lost Shakers?" she asks, nodding to where the old dudes are doing shots of tequila at the bar.

"Jeff Bridges, for sure," I say, squinting.

"Okay, okay, I can see that," Elise says.

"What about the waiter?"

"Um," Elise says, slurping all the cheese and toppings off her pizza first, a habit that makes me crazy. "Maybe like a Will Smith thing going?"

"No way," I say, watching him scratch his nose at the servers' station. "One of the extras on the set of a Will Smith movie, maybe." This makes Elise laugh until she snorts, and then for a few moments the air is clear between us, none of the usual dustups clouding the evening.

"What about Liam?" Elise asks. Liam looks like nobody but himself, though I don't want to say such a thing out loud. But even this question doesn't derail us, because the band interrupts, tuning their instruments and checking their mics. We pay our bill so we can stand on the dance floor, where a few other people are milling around with drinks in their hands. I sip at my root beer, wishing again that I hadn't chosen to wear a cardigan.

"Hello, Mercer!" Liam yells as though he's welcoming a stadium full of fans. "We are the Straitjackets!"

I'm not completely sure what I expected from the band, but when the first song begins, I have to fight the urge to cover my ears. It is not merely loud; it is belligerently loud, combatively loud. The drum, in particular, seems to be intent on assaulting me, pounding for entrance against the tightly locked door of my sternum. I can tell by the way the guitarist's fingers are moving that what he is attempting is not easy, but the effort is not borne out in the sound. The bassist seems utterly glazed over, not entirely aware of what is happening. As for Liam, I'd had a vague notion of him as a good singer dating back to the days when we were children, when he did silly parodies of pop songs for the radio show. And there are moments now, when he is actually singing, when it sounds okay, but there are a lot of other sounds emanating from his mouth, growls and grunts and rasps and screams. The whole thing is a little like an angry patchwork quilt: strangely pieced together, sort of ugly, and capable of smothering.

I look around the room, trying to gauge the crowd. About half of the audience members seem to be genuinely enjoying themselves, and the other half appear to feel the same way I do. Across the room, I can see an older guy in a polo shirt twisting up pieces of a cocktail napkin and screwing them into his ears. A few people with more tact drift out the doors to the back patio, where the volleyball game is still in progress. Elise is having fun, though I'm not certain that the music is having its intended effect on her. She is dancing enthusiastically, sometimes head-banging or throwing up metal horns, but also doing a hodgepodge of moves that are wildly incongruent with the music: the Robot, the Hustle, the Charleston. She hands me her drink and bounces up and down like a cheerleader. A couple songs in, she's sipping at the beer of some older kid who I think might have graduated from our school last year. Brandon? Benjamin? Something like that. The room is getting more crowded and Elise pushes toward the stage, and I use it as a convenient opportunity to hang back, slightly apart from her.

And then, at the start of the next song, Liam searches the audience until his eyes fall upon me. "This song is for Anna, who thinks I'm hot," he breathes into the microphone. I can't make my throat work well enough to swallow. A few people look at me, and Elise looks over her shoulder and then pumps her fist into the air, laughing and cheering. For a moment I want to disappear, but I forget myself a little when I realize that the first bars of the song are beautiful: the guitar player softly braiding together a series of arpeggios against the soulful crooning tenor of Liam's voice.

"Days when you can't even see to the center of yourself," he sings, and the melancholy tune of it is so in harmony with how I walk through the world that I can feel some more obstinate, judgmental part of me give way to pure feeling.

When we were little, there was a little bit of tragedy hanging around Liam. Elise's cousin Julian, Liam's brother, died when we were still little kids. Sometimes I used to imagine that while I was sitting in the emergency room, death passing me by after I fell from the window, Julian was upstairs in the cancer ward, doomed. I used to think this imagined story was proof of the connection between me and Liam, and though I mostly consider that kind of superstitious thinking to be long behind me, in this moment, listening to Liam sing to me, I almost believe in it again.

The song hangs in suspension for a moment, and then the drum breaks the spell with a terrible, earsplitting crash and the band members leap around the stage and Liam screams something like "Impenetrable fog!" into the microphone, though who could really know with every instrument competing to be the loudest? The shift in the song seems like a joke that has been played on me, and whatever enthusiasm I've mustered for this evening hits the brakes and rolls to a complete stop.

6

TO THE RIGHT

ANNA TURNS OUT OF the funeral home parking lot and hits the gas, and the air-conditioning pours over me like a wave. It wakes up something in my sluggish blood, makes me feel more like myself. I fiddle with the stereo, switching from the CD she had been playing to the local classic rock station, and she doesn't stop me. The radio stations are shit in this town, but sometimes this one plays okay stuff. I listen to a few seconds of Ozzy singing about being turned to steel in a great magnetic field. Perfect.

"Where are we going?" I ask.

"You were the one who suggested this. I thought you'd think of something."

"Hmm. An opium den, maybe? High tea at the Waldorf?

Or, you know, I hear there's a hot wake going on somewhere near here."

She is not exactly smiling, but her mouth is turned up slightly at the corners. "Well, we're going here, then, I guess," she says, and takes an abrupt right into the parking lot of a small ice cream shop. Even on a hot day, no one is getting ice cream this close to dinnertime; the two picnic tables out front are empty. We can't be more than a couple miles from the funeral home, but it feels as remote as a desert island.

"My treat," I say as we climb out of the car, "for getting me away from there. What do you want?"

"Mmm," she says, giving it serious thought. "What are you having?"

It's a no-brainer for me. "Butter pecan."

She looks offended. "That's an old person's flavor. Seriously, when a car full of old people pull in here, I know they're all going to order butter pecan."

"You work here?"

"A few nights a week. Just for the summer. I'll have cookies and cream."

"Cone or a cup?"

"You're killing me here. Cups are for amateurs. If you order butter pecan in a cup, I might get back in the car and ditch you."

Are we flirting? I can't tell, but I like that she's turned a little bit prickly. It's better than that gray void on her face when her eyes were closed.

The curly-haired boy at the window looks about twelve. He says hello to Anna and gives us our cones for free, and then we take a look at the sad, empty benches dotted with ice cream stains.

"Wanna walk while we eat?" Anna asks.

We wander across the parking lot, toward the squat little building next door that serves as the local news radio station, and work for a few minutes on consuming our ice cream before the drip of melt-off reaches our hands. Her elbow jostles against mine, and I like being so close to her, even if she's not exactly my type.

"So you and Elise were tight," I say finally, when I've eaten down to the lip of the cone.

"Yeah." She pauses. "Haven't seen much of her this summer, though."

I nod. I feel like telling her that she doesn't have to feel guilty about that, but I also know that she will anyway, no matter what some stranger says. Grief is a wily little demon, for sure.

Anna sighs. "Elise is one of those people who wants to do a million things at once, but I didn't have a choice except to focus, really focus, on violin, or I'd never make it to statewide orchestra. She just didn't get it. She wanted me to be her playmate, like I used to be. And now what? She didn't get what she wanted. I didn't get what I wanted. Now she's gone, and there's no way to fix it." She stops abruptly, looking slightly embarrassed by this waterfall of words.

47

"Life is fucking garrrrbage," I sing, trying to make her feel better, and then I hold the remainder of the cone in my mouth so I can play an air guitar riff. "That's from my new hit single 'Life Is Fucking Garbage.'"

A real smile flits briefly over her features, and I'm surprised at how it transforms her face; her eyes are a different shape, and there's the trace of a dimple on her right cheek. She's pretty; I can see it now. I've known girls like Anna before, girls who are so serious that they wear it like a suit of armor. Maybe, though, I've just never been around at the right moment to see the armor dropped.

"Definitely," she says, but she's noticed my gaze and goes quiet, looking down at her ice cream, up at the radio tower on the far side of the news station, anywhere but in my direction.

"That orchestra is no joke," I say. I sang alongside them last year, when the statewide choir gave a combined Christmas concert with them, but I don't mention this. "I'm sorry it didn't work out."

She doesn't answer right away. We've reached the metal fence that surrounds the radio tower, and Anna sits on the ground in a little patch of shade, leans against the fence. I sit beside her, close enough that I can feel the brush of her upper arm next to mine.

"The tryout is tomorrow," she says. "I can't go."

"Why not?" I ask, then realize I already know the answer.

"The funeral. All she wanted was me, my time. I can't..."

She stops and looks at the sky. "I just can't. And please don't tell me that she'd want me to be happy or that she'll never know anyway or any of the other idiotic things that people have said to me over the past few days."

"Jesus. 'She'll never know anyway'? Someone really said that?"

Anna nods, covers her face with her hands. "My violin teacher. He's the worst."

"Hey, was that the piece you were going to play? The one you were listening to in the car?"

She nods again, her face still hidden. The way she's curling into herself, trying to disappear—I recognize it. She's probably never had someone close to her die, and if that's the case, she's about to learn some of the shit I'm unlucky enough to already know—about how loss feels like the center of gravity in your universe for years and years after it happens.

"It was pretty," I say with a not-good-enough attempt at kindness.

She drops her hands and looks at me, scornful. "Pretty? It's not pretty. Paganini was so fierce that people said he was in league with the devil. He was refused a Christian burial. That piece is like a...a plane crash. Like a human sacrifice."

I smile at her. "That's great. I'm going to write a song tonight, and I'm going to try to make it sound like a plane crash."

"You better name it after me," she says.

"Sure. Anna's Song, colon, A Human Sacrifice."

The ice cream is gone, but we let a few more minutes tick by while the sun sinks lower and starts to turn the clouds coral. The world always carpet-bombs you with its natural beauty when you least feel like acknowledging it. I broke up with Muriel for the final time last fall under the most extraordinary red maple tree. In my memory, the tree is not merely scarlet, but engulfed in flames.

"Would they make an exception for you?" I finally ask. "Let you audition later?"

"Maybe," she says. "But the idea of playing makes me feel sick. Like actually physically ill. I haven't been able to practice since I heard."

I tilt my head back. The radio tower looms above us like some sort of spacecraft, the tip of it piercing the sky. I know logically that it's only a dinky local tower with minimal range, but here in its shadow, it feels ominous, like it could transport us beyond Earth's atmosphere, leaving no trace behind.

"I'm Elise's best friend, but I can't cry at her wake," Anna says. "I'm a violinist, but I can't play violin. I'm an anti-person."

"Bullshit," I say. "You're no less of a person because you don't want to play violin. I mean that. Being good at something isn't the same as wanting to do it."

She shrugs.

"I'm not going to do any of the school choir stuff this year," I confess. "I want to focus on my own music."

"I wish I could do the same," Anna says. "Violin used to feel like my destiny, and now..." She sighs. "Do you ever feel like you somehow got dropped into the wrong life?"

Something sparks in my gut, and now there's electricity running through my blood. Maybe we are mirror images, the two of us. Maybe it is kismet, a magical convergence that we ended up right here, right now, though I don't know what it means yet. Are there death metal bands with violin players?

"Maybe you *should* do the same. Play fiddle in a rock band or something. Forge your own path."

"Fiddle?" she asks, raising one eyebrow. "It's hard to imagine a future in which I am a *fiddle* player."

"Well, okay, then." I laugh. "I guess I got ahead of myself." The flame gutters a little, but it doesn't go out. It has to mean something that we are both musicians, both searching for a new way to make art. I don't believe in God, not after what happened to Julian, but I do think there must be some great force that powers existence, and didn't that same force draw us together? I have a strong desire to interlace my fingers with hers, to feel the cool skin of her palm again. I sit on my hand to keep myself from doing something embarrassing.

"What's your music like?" she asks.

"It's, um, a 'barbaric yawp over the roofs of the world,'" I say. I feel suddenly shy about the kind of music I make, and then the utter lameness of that fact fills me with frustration.

"It's not everybody's thing. But maybe it's *your* thing. You should come to our show this weekend and find out."

"Hmm," she says. "Give me a preview."

"Here?"

She looks me in the eye and smiles, and I feel that current beneath the surface of my skin once again. "Greatness exceeds context," she says.

I can't argue with that. I close my eyes and fill my lungs and let loose the final few bars of "Dusk All Day." I imagine the tower beaming my voice up, up, over the land and toward the stars. "Ruination 'til the end, my friends," I sing, and when I open my eyes, she is blinking at me, a little startled, and I experience a swirl of vertigo, unable to fully fathom what we're doing here.

"Bravissimo," she says, and laughs, a real laugh, but the way she's looking at me, I know she's not laughing at me. "That was extraordinary. The best performance this parking lot has ever seen."

For a split second, it's as though I can feel every particle in my body and in hers too, vibrating, colliding into one another.

"We should go," Anna says.

"I guess so," I say, reluctant to leave behind the here and now, this strangely satisfying moment. The Golden Hour, that's what photographers call this time, and everything looks better in it. But I get up, follow her back to the car, watch her brush the dried grass from the seat of her skirt, try to seal the loveliness of the gesture into my memory.

On the road, we're uneasy again. She asks for the details of the show; I give them to her. I scan through the radio stations, but only to give my hands something to do. And then, right before she pulls back into the parking lot of the funeral home, she says, "It doesn't seem possible that the world goes right on existing without her."

"Yeah," I say, because I've spent most of my life existing in a place of absence, a negative space, and I know what she's saying. "There's this thing in quantum physics," I say as she eases the car back into the same spot where she was parked before. "It says that there are zillions of copies of the universe, countless variations. It means there are other worlds in which Elise never got into a car accident. And others in which she never existed at all."

"Huh," Anna says.

I don't know what made me go into all that; it's something I keep tucked away usually, just for me. She puts the car in park but doesn't turn off the engine. There are goose bumps on her forearm, where the sleeve of her dress ends, and I wonder if it might be because of what I told her about Many Worlds. Either that or the air-conditioning, which is still turned up much too high. Then she says, "Do you believe that? Do you think that's how it works?"

"I don't know," I tell her honestly. "I guess it doesn't matter much, because either way, we're stuck here. It's not like we can pick the best universe to live in."

"Yeah." She leans her head against the seat. "I don't think I can go back in there right now. But I'll see you at the funeral tomorrow."

"Unless you decide to go to the audition."

Her eyes, which I previously thought were brown, are really a mix of green and gold and coffee; they are earthy like a pond reflecting the evening rays of the sun. I could let myself fall into them, float there.

"Probably not in this universe," she says.

Back in the room with Elise's coffin, most of the teachers and students have cleared out. When I cross the room to put my arm around Aunt Caroline, my dad walks up behind me to say through gritted teeth, "Where have you been?" It doesn't matter, though. The taste of ice cream is still on my tongue and the memory of Anna in the golden light is still on my mind, and I feel like maybe something in the world has shifted.

7

TO THE LEFT

AFTER THE SHOW, ELISE volunteers us to help with the band's gear. My ears are still ringing while I drag some part of the drum kit seemingly made of lead to the parking lot. Elise is carrying only two cables around her neck and talking to the blond bassist in a giggly, conspiratorial way.

I offload my burden into the back of the drummer's van and then, trying to be nice, I smile awkwardly at Liam, who is guzzling from a water bottle a few yards away.

"Nice job up there," I say.

Liam turns to smile at me. I can't quite identify the flavor of the smile. "Well, thanks. You looked like you were having a real blast."

Oh, I see now: sarcasm.

"Sorry," I mumble.

"Hey, no problem." He points at me with the bottle. "Have we met before?"

I fold my arms as though I'm cold, trying to squeeze myself together. "I used to see you at Elise's house all the time when we were little kids."

"Huh." He walks a little closer, studying my face until I don't know what to do but stare at the ground. "Nope, I don't remember."

I feel a little kick of anger in my gut at this, but it's mostly aimed at me; I'm mad at myself for remembering him with such crystal clarity and for craving his approval, then and now.

I look over to where Elise is still talking to the bassist. They're smoking something together, probably weed. Great. I hate having to have conversations with Elise when she's stoned, the looping emptiness of them. To get away from Liam, I go back inside and head to the bathroom before I collect another armload of equipment.

In a stall that is full of drunken graffiti, I take my time, running the orchestra audition through my head again, rewinding it like a video.

I *have* to get in. With a state-level performing group on my resume, there's still a chance at a really good conservatory, maybe even Juilliard. It's more than that, though. Sometimes I think that trying, really trying, and coming up short is the worst thing that could happen to me, and despite knowing that's not really true, it *feels* true, down in my gut.

Eventually I use the anemic hand dryer and drag myself back toward the stage for more equipment, even though lifting anything with my left hand causes a little thunderclap of pain in my wrist that vibrates up my arm. It's on my way back to the van that I notice a group of adults a little younger than my parents eating pizza together at a table near the back door, and my violin teacher is sitting right there on the end. I try to hurry past, not wanting to engage, but then I hear someone say my name and I reluctantly turn to see Mr. Foster out of his seat, walking toward me.

How this moment makes me long for stately Mrs. Oslo, who was my violin teacher from fifth grade until last year, when she finally dropped her last few students and retired definitively. Mrs. Oslo had worsening arthritis and a shaky memory, but she always gave me a butterscotch candy at the end of the lesson, and she never would have insisted that I call her by her first name. Now I'm stuck with Call-Me-Gary. I know I should be grateful. He performed for several years with the Philadelphia Philharmonic and now plays in the Cleveland Symphony and a bunch of other ensembles. He's one of the most talented musicians ever to come from this town, and the fact that he lives here again is really nothing more than a fluke—an obligation to ailing parents that I've heard about only in vague snippets of gossip. When we play together, I sometimes feel lifted (or at least dragged along by) the power of his sound. And yet...he is always impatient with my mistakes, always cutting me off when I try to ask him a question, always staring at me like he's more interested in watching me than listening to me.

In short, I don't really like him.

And now here he is, slinging an arm around me before I even have time to set down a cymbal case. He smells of too-strong cologne and beer.

"Did you get the letter?" he asks. "I know you must be ecstatic."

"Letter?" I say, but my heart is already flapping its butter-fly wings and rising up, up out of my chest.

Call-Me-Gary turns to his table of friends and points to me. "Anna here is the me of her generation. But with a bet-ter body." The men at the table smirk and look down at their beers, and the two women with them groan and roll their eyes. One of them throws a balled-up napkin at him. They're all drunk, I realize then. I duck out from under his arm, and it makes him lose his footing for a second.

"What letter?" I ask again.

"I got the list today," Call-Me-Gary says, still swaying slightly. "You're the only one from the school to make state this year. And the first violin section is not easy to get into as a junior."

And then I don't really care that Call-Me-Gary is icky and an embarrassment to himself; it feels almost good when he claps me on the shoulder and congratulates me. The first thing that springs to my lips to say is, "Now I'm a real person," but I'm so embarrassed by this impulse that I say instead, "Thank you. I didn't know. Thank you for telling me." And then I grab the gear and hurry off to the parking lot to find Elise.

I feel as if I could ride the cymbal case like a surfboard on the waves of pure glee that are now rolling through me. Elise is still smoking with the bassist, but now I'm too happy to care that she's ignoring me.

"What's up?" Liam asks. He's sitting on the bumper of the van, and I can't help it—I'm grinning like a maniac. "You look like you took a hit of laughing gas while you were in there."

"It's nothing. An orchestra I really wanted to get into—they liked my audition."

"Statewide?" Liam asks, standing up and stretching non-chalantly. Something about his closeness makes me anxious. The exhilaration that filled my chest curls back into my heart like a cautious sea creature retracting into its shell. He says, "I did statewide choir last year, but I'm not sure I'm going to accept again this year. The drive down to Columbus once a week for rehearsal is kind of a drag, you know?"

I swallow hard. The drive is nothing, the seat in the orchestra everything. I feel robbed of the joy that is due to me at this moment of victory. Screw him. I shove the case into the back of the van. If there's one small grace in all this, it's that Liam is still bent over, stretching his fingers toward his toes, so that he can't see the angry tears that are pricking at my eyes. I have always cried easily, a tendency that humiliates me but that I cannot seem to control. Elise comes bounding over and leaps onto Liam's leveled back.

"Hey, cuz," she says. "That show rocked. I'm so glad I came."

Liam grabs her arms, pinning her to his back, and then stands up, spinning around as Elise laughs like a little kid. There will be no talking to her about the orchestra tonight, I guess; I wonder if it will ever feel like there's enough room in Elise's world for me to be more than her sidekick. After Liam deposits her back on the ground, he says, "We could be so much better if those guys would just try for once. But thanks for coming out. Any chance you can give me a lift home?"

"Sure, sure, sure," Elise says, grinning stupidly. "Noooo problem."

I pluck the keys from Elise's purse in one swift motion. "I'll drive," I say. "Your mom will never let you out of the house again if you get another ticket."

Another of our recurring arguments is about me being too uptight and bossy, but this time Elise only smiles sheepishly. "Ain't that the truth, Anna banana? Let's go."

"Shotgun," Liam calls, then shouts a farewell to his bandmates with some kind of Scandinavian nonsense thrown in.

I pull the release on the driver's seat, moving it forward and letting Elise burrow into the tiny back seat of the car. When we're all in, Elise leans far forward between the two front seats and lays her head first on Liam's shoulder and then on mine. Her body spasms with a shiver as I turn the key in the ignition. "Whew, someone must be walking on my grave, guys," she says, and then laughs.

Liam lives in the opposite direction as Elise and I do, and I am suddenly bone tired. I wish for immediate teleportation to bed, but the wish goes ungranted. I wish I could kick Liam out of the car, leave him on the side of the road, but this, too, seems unlikely. I roll down the window to try to catch a breeze and wake up a little.

"Guys," Elise says, poking her head into the front seat again. "Look how beautiful the stars are tonight. Do you think they'd be this beautiful if we weren't here to see them?" She giggles.

"Sometimes I think they're too perfect-looking," Liam says. "Like someone is trying to fool us with a stage set or something."

"Whoa, crazy," Elise says. "Like that movie. What's it called?"

The stars have always looked like sheet music in negative to me, like notes that are running wild over an entire sky instead of being confined to a staff. I wonder sometimes what it would sound like if someone were able to play them, if someone could sight-read the song of the universe.

Elise sighs. "This is so great, being with the two of you. What if the three of us had stayed close after Liam moved out here?"

"There's this thing called the Many Worlds theory," Liam says. He points to a neighborhood coming up on the right. "Turn in here. It says that there are zillions of copies of the universe, countless variations. It means that in another world, we're all best friends. Wouldn't you love that, Anna banana?"

I refuse to look at him, not wanting to see the caustic grin on his admittedly gorgeous face. His theory sounds empty and dumb, or at least like it's been impossibly diluted by someone who likes the dreamy idea of it more than he understands the science behind it. But if it's true, if there's a parade of other Annas living other lives, I want there to be a universe in which I don't have to constantly wonder if I'm good enough.

//

I feel a strong kinship with parallel Maxes, even though I never get to meet them. They share my values, my feelings, my memories—they're closer to me than brothers.

—MAX TEGMARK, quantum physicist

8

TO THE RIGHT

NOT A WORD PASSED between Anna and me on the day of Elise's funeral, though I kept noticing little things about her from across the room: the freckle on the left side of her neck; the extremely upright posture that she shares with her mother, who was sitting next to her; the barest whiff of her perfume or maybe shampoo that I got when she walked past me at the end, giving a small wave goodbye. There was part of me that wanted to find some way for us to escape together again, to run away from the flowers and black dresses and sadness. But there's another part of me that can't quite imagine us ever dating. She is so, so different from Muriel, with more than a little bit of zipped-up nerdiness about her. *She's not my type*, I kept telling myself that day, but then would find myself studying some part of her—her full, serious lips, her long fingers, the slope of her shoulder.

Now here she is, looking too classy for this stupid pizza place, sitting alone at a small table near the back. While getting ready for our set, the possibility that she might show up was all I could think about, and now she is here in the flesh, the gentle curve of that lower lip pursed around a straw.

I decide to make eye contact with her while singing, to communicate some felt connection between us, but when I'm standing at the microphone, I can't make myself engage with her, and I take refuge in the music instead, shelter in the act of performing. My stomach feels like two hamsters fighting for control of the same wheel, a clue that somehow, this girl has gotten under my skin more than anyone since Muriel showed up as the new girl in ninth grade. (God, she was beautiful—I spent most of every Geometry class studying that scant but alluring slice of skin where her sweater didn't quite meet her jeans.)

"This song is for Anna, who accepts my failings in matters of ice cream," I breathe into the microphone, hoping this little inside joke will make her smile. While I sing the opening bars of "Impenetrable Fog," I steal a look at her through my eyelashes, and she's listening so intently. It's the prettiest of all our songs.

We race through our set list, making it to the end quickly if not gracefully, and Anna approaches the stage looking almost happy, full of compliments about the show and offering to help us load out the equipment. I manage to bum a ride home with her; among other things, it allows me to escape Chris and Eric. They'd made every imaginable mistake onstage—missed entrances, bumbled tempos, both of them letting fly pitchy notes like unrestrained belches. When Anna tells me again that she enjoyed the show, I brush it off, embarrassed. She shifts the car into park in my driveway and then touches my hand and says, "No, really. You're talented, and it doesn't take a genius to see it."

I look at our hands stacked, two rafts atop each other, feeling the pull of the current. "We could be so much better if those guys would just try for once."

"So be a solo act. Your music is *your* music; isn't that what you were telling me? You don't have to share it with them if you don't want to."

I want to kiss her then, but I don't. Maybe I'm too chickenshit to take a chance on something unfamiliar. I watch the movement of her heartbeat in the soft curve of her neck. I take my hand from under hers and give her shoulder a squeeze, like some friendly guidance counselor. Awful. My legs feel wooden as I lurch from the car. That's it; it's done. I've missed the boat, and it will never pass this shore again. Bon voyage.

I did, of course, manage to kiss Muriel by the end of our freshman year. When I learned that she was into photography, I took her out to an abandoned railroad bridge, and she one-upped me by crawling out on the trusses to take photos of the ravine below. I almost blacked out from terror, but I followed her, and then we kissed, both of us suspended in midair, just a foot in either direction from certain death. I let her convince me that I liked that rush of adrenaline, that it was more than heart-crushing fear that I was feeling, and then I continued to let her and probably lots of other people believe that I'm too cool to be bothered by the idea of death. Only I know the truth: I was a coward then, and I'm a coward still.

Anna backs the car into the quiet street, but before she drives away into the darkness and out of my life, she rolls down the window and calls to me, "Hey, do you want to hang out sometime? Talk about nerdy music stuff?"

Very occasionally, fortune favors even a coward like me.

A few days later, I pick her up from one of her last shifts of the season at the ice cream shop, and we drive to the quiet park that I usually stop at on my way to Gavin's house. This is my secret hideaway where I work on lyrics, where I mutter rhymes and bellow ideas into the unbiased air. I've never shared its location with anyone, but it seems right to take another serious musician there.

The drive here felt a little too much like a first date, inherently awkward, and all wrong to be in my father's too-nice SUV instead of the aging sedan she'd driven to Elise's wake.

Once we get to the park and sit down, though (civilly, on separate boulders, me offering the taller, more comfortable rock to her), we relax a little. She pilfered some of the candy that the shop uses to top ice cream sundaes. While we eat it, I tell her a story about M&M'S, about how when I was around seven or eight, I'd learned the term *super-taster* and informed my parents that I could identify the color of the M&M'S by the subtle differences in the flavor of the dyes. They'd humored me, putting the candies in my mouth and pretending not to notice when I stole peeks at the color through my eyelashes. (That was back in the days when my parents were still straining to see me as extraordinary, an effort that they eventually dropped.)

I am beginning to wonder why in the world I have fallen into telling her such an idiotic story, when she says, "That's sweet. There should be more songs about things like that, I think: the tiny, specific memories that make your life feel like your own."

That makes me laugh. "I'm not sure how to rhyme M&M with anything."

"You think I'm kidding, but I'm serious," she says. "And 'feminine' almost rhymes."

I have no interest in writing a song about M&M'S or my parents, but I do allow my mind to wander through a few pleasant recollections from childhood: my mother snuggling next to Julian and me on the couch to read us a story, the soft worn fleece of my favorite stuffed animal, Mr. Peeps the Sheep, against my cheek, the smell of snickerdoodles baking in my aunt's kitchen. Something about Anna makes me want to tell her all of this, even though I never talk to anyone about Julian, not even Muriel, not even at our closest.

But Anna is talking now, a story about a time she ate too many Junior Mints the first time her mother took her to see *The Nutcracker*, about how she now associates the sick, heavy feeling with looking up at her mother during the "Dance of the Sugar Plum Fairy" and seeing her eyes welling with tears. "When I asked her about it later, she said, 'Oh, Anna, it was because they were too beautiful,' but even as a child, I knew that it had more to do with her not being able to dance any-more." Anna talks a lot with her hands, and I wonder if she does it on purpose, if she knows how exquisite they are.

"Damn," I say. "That one really is a song."

"It would have to be a violin song," Anna says. "I can't sing." And then in a jokingly deep voice, she warbles, "And that's the Junior Mints bluuuuues."

We laugh, but the laughter gives way to another moment in which I wonder briefly if she wants me to kiss her, but it is awkward because of the different levels of our respective rocks, and while I am pondering a smooth way around this obstacle, I let the conversation languish in an unnecessarily uncomfortable pause, and she is already trying to fill it with small talk, her eyes avoiding mine.

"Does your band have any more shows coming up?" she asks.

"Nah," I say. I don't bother to explain the whiny, complaining phone call I got from Chris yesterday, giving me ridiculous ultimatums about showcasing his guitar skills on more songs or accepting that I'd have to find a new guitar player. I had said simply, "Okay," and hung up on him. The truth is, I don't want to do the work to find a new guitar player, so we will eventually spend a rehearsal listening to Chris noodle around on sprawling solos that add little to the songs they land in. But first there will be a week in which none of us speak to one another while Chris and I stew over the argument and Eric parties with his other friends and Gavin does whatever it is he does—hand-carve new drumsticks from the wood of a tree he's meditatively felled by himself or something. It is the same pattern as always, and it makes me feel so, so tired.

But rather than try to make Anna understand any of that, I say, "I bet you're a way better musician than any of them."

"Well," she says, "I am a better violinist than any of them, I'm pretty sure."

She's only joking, but she's right: Here is talent, real talent, right in front of me, and there is no logical reason to fool around with amateurs instead of finding a way to intertwine my skill with hers. Who cares if she doesn't want to be in a rock band? Who cares if I've never actually heard her play the violin?

"Let's write music together," I say. "Let's tell each other more stories and then see if we can grow them into songs."

She opens her mouth as though to protest, then shuts it again, thinking. Her hand moves against her leg in an absent-minded vibrato. "It wouldn't be like a normal band," she says finally. "With only a violinist and a singer...I'm not sure what it would be, actually."

I smile at her. "Who wants to be easy to define, anyway?"

"Okay," she says, looking as purely happy as I've yet seen her, and it feels like the beginning of something good.

A few days later, we're sitting in Anna's living room, trying to stir up some magic. The reality of starting the project, how-ever, is a little bit of a comedown from the giddy anticipa-tion of it. Nothing is ever as perfect as that moment when it springs to life as an idea, no matter how much I want it to be.

And yet, we are trying, and I can feel that she wants it to work as much as I do, and maybe that alone is enough. This is the first time, at least as far as I know, that she's played in front of anyone since Elise died. There is nothing gingerly or delicate about the way she handles the instrument; it is no-nonsense, almost brusque, and it broadcasts a smooth confidence. It is very, very sexy.

"You know," she says, "if I'd auditioned for the orchestra,

I'd be driving to the first rehearsal right now. If I'd gotten in, I mean."

"You would have," I say, because I really don't doubt it. "Does it make you sad? Not being there?"

"Not exactly," she says. "It feels far away. Like that was a different lifetime." She recently dropped out of her school orchestra and kicked her private teacher to the curb; she told me this last week, in an almost whisper, like she was confessing a dark secret.

Anna takes a long, deliberate breath, as though she is about to plunge into cold water. "Now what?"

"Now you find the song that I know is inside of you, and you play it," I say. "And I fall to my knees in awe."

She smiles at me. "No pressure or anything."

"Right. No pressure."

Anna starts messing around a little, running up and down scales, playing scraps of other songs like a radio trying to find the right frequency. And then she settles into a melody, a sliding chain of notes in a minor key that resolve themselves at the last second into a major chord.

"That's good," I say. "Damn, that's really good." She stops, tucks her violin under her arm, tucks her hair behind her ear. "No, don't stop now!" I say, but she shakes her head and takes a step back.

"That little fragment came to me while I was getting

dressed this morning, but I'm not sure where it goes next," she says. I am momentarily distracted by the thought of her getting dressed, the soft cotton of her T-shirt sliding over her bra and her smooth skin. She flops onto the couch, agitating the mop of a dog that has settled itself on the far corner. It blinks its milky eyes at her and whines softly before tucking its nose back under its rear leg. I'm allergic—I could feel my eyes begin to itch before the dog even made an appearance— but I haven't wanted to mention it.

"Sorry, Twyla," she says.

I hum the melody she played, trying to hold on to it. "What were you thinking about when it first came to you?"

Her face tightens for a moment. "Elise, I guess. It's still hard to think about much else."

"Tell me a story about Elise, then. One of the memories you've been thinking about."

She groans and strokes the patch of fur between the dog's eyes, but she doesn't refuse, and I wait.

"All right. Once, on a snow day, I walked all the way to Elise's house to help her build a snow castle in the backyard. This is when we were...I don't know, maybe nine? When I got there, Elise had a few rectangular plastic bins that she'd gotten somewhere and she packed snow into them and poured water over it and then turned out blocks that were really hard and icy. It was sort of ingenious, really, like a mammoth ice cube tray. I was amazed by it."

"Because you wouldn't have thought of that?"

"Right. You know Elise. She was a million times more inventive than anyone else around. Anyway, she got bored of it before we finished a single wall, and she insisted that we go sledding instead, at that big hill near the back of her neighborhood. All the kids used to call it Kamikaze Hill because it was so steep and there were so many trees to steer around at the bottom. I didn't want to go. But you know how Elise could be."

"Say it out loud. How could she be?"

Anna glances at me, frowning at the lame therapist-style questions.

"Sorry," I say. "Sometimes you just have to keep talking until you find the lyrics."

Anna scratches Twyla's ears, and her back paw pounds the couch in response. "Elise was unpredictable. And she was usually determined to have her way, pushy about it, right up to the edge of meanness." She pauses, and I can tell she's a little uncomfortable, but I like that she's being honest about Elise. I never thought of Elise as pushy, but I can believe that Anna did, and I hate fakery more than anything. "She nagged me into climbing to the top of the hill, *just to see*, and I let her do it, because I didn't want to turn around and walk all the way home. I'd spent half an hour walking over there in the snow, not even counting the time it took to talk my mom into letting me go alone. And then when we got up there, I watched her go down the hill a couple times, and she said that I should sit on her sled, *just to see*."

I already know the type of thing that is coming next. There is something fragile about Anna that invites a low-grade destructive impulse, even in me. It's like the urge to pull a cat's tail, but only one that you're pretty sure isn't going to scratch you in return. I feel a little tendril of shame unfurl in me but try to ignore it and focus on what she's saying.

"So I sat on the sled, and then I felt a push from behind, and it not only sent me racing down the hill, but it knocked me off-balance so I couldn't steer. I ran into a tree, hard, and it chipped the corner off my left front tooth. I remember sitting up and reaching inside my mouth and plucking this tiny white triangle off my tongue."

Behind her closed lips, her tongue is momentarily sliding over the tooth in question. Her tongue, her teeth, her perfect lips—I clear my throat unnecessarily.

"Elise came running, of course, and I remember how wide and scared her eyes were, but I just said, 'I have to go,' and took off running. Somewhere, I'd heard that if you cut your finger off, you have to take it to the hospital to reattach it, so I thought if I could run home fast enough with my tooth fragment, everything would be okay. I dropped it when I was halfway there and couldn't find it in the snow, and that's when I burst into tears."

"Shit," I say. "*That's* what you've been thinking about Elise? Why'd you stay friends with her, then?"

"That's not the important part, actually," Anna says. She takes a deep breath, and I can see that she's working to tell the story the right way, and this time the vulnerability makes me want to protect her, which is a lot easier to take. "My parents couldn't take me to the dentist until the next day, because the roads were so bad, but when we did finally get there, it was fine. I remember Dr. Ganhurst humming a tune while he worked in my mouth, and he said to me, 'Don't worry, cookie. People chip their teeth all the time.' And he put a cap on my tooth, and you can't even really tell it was chipped. So no big deal.

"Here's the main thing, though: When I got home, Elise was in our backyard, building a castle. I was still too mad at her, and I didn't want to go out there, even though my mom kept telling me to go outside and tell her that my tooth had been fixed. Elise kept at it all day, until it got dark, and then she left without ever knocking on the door. I went out there then, to look at it. It was this giant cube with a tarp for a roof and a plank for a door and two chairs built out of ice inside, and in the snow next to the chairs, she'd written, 'Sorry I was mean to you.' We never talked about any of it, we never sat in the ice chairs together, but the snow was so tightly packed that it remained standing for weeks, long after everything else had melted."

I can easily see Elise, out there in the snow, heaving blocks that were almost as big as her. "She did like a big gesture," I

77

say. "She once splattered red paint all over a T-shirt with a turkey on it and wore it to our family Thanksgiving to protest our wanton killing of America's greatest bird."

"Yeah, that sounds right," Anna says. She lifts the violin to her shoulder, plays the same melody as before, almost too softly to be heard, with the tiniest little motions of the bow. "I always think of Elise as being indecisive, but maybe it was more that she could let things go easily. When I'm right, I can feel it, and I clamp down on it, I sink my teeth into it. I think most people are like that. But she didn't hold on to her rightness like that, or her wrongness, either."

"So that's what the story is about to you?"

Anna frowns and plays the same snippet of melody again. "Yeah, it was a big gesture, like you said. But it was also a way of getting both of us past her mistake, a way of not letting us get stuck there. It's one of the things I miss most about her." She plays the phrase a third time, but this time, she keeps going, finding the next part of the melody, letting the volume grow until finally she hits an abrupt dissonant note—not a mistake, but an exclamation of discontent.

"I'm afraid of getting stuck here without her," Anna says without meeting my gaze.

I want to reach out and hold her, to console her or commiserate with her, because I know that fear of being alone, of having to struggle to be a whole person when you feel like something has been subtracted from you. More than that, though, I want to pump my fist in the air like an idiot, I want to shout from the rooftops, because what she just did, unearthing a memory that gives rise to its own melody, is beautiful and full of artistry. It's what I'm always reaching for when I write songs but rarely get to grasp. I've only been sitting here listening, but my heart is pounding and my neck is sweaty. This, it's the thing that's been sorely lacking from all the interactions with the band, that racing feeling of joyous creation.

But instead of making any move at all, I hold very, very still, trying not to startle the newborn song, treating it like a skittish deer. I wait until she plays the whole melody again, and this time I hum along with it.

"I think I almost have it," she says, brow furrowed.

"One more time?" I ask. And this time, I try singing a few lines: "Cold as the way an ice crystal grows, cold as the way the days seem to slow."

This time when she hits that final note, she looks at me and smiles, and I'd bet a million dollars that our hearts are beating in sync, and then we both giggle like little kids at how good it all feels. Behind that classical exterior, she is a rock star. I knew it before, but now I'm certain. This is art and beauty and life, all of it pressed together and expanding inside me like the explosion that results in a star.

I want to take her hands in mine, and I rise, ready for it, my arms already outstretched, but then we hear the front door open, and then her mom is in the room, like an emissary from a different planet.

"Oh, hello," she says to the stranger in her living room. We both stare at her dumbly until she extends a graceful hand and says, "I'm Anna's mother."

"This is Liam," Anna says hurriedly as I shake her mother's hand and Twyla rouses herself and jumps tenderly off the couch. Then she blurts: "He's a musical genius." Anna's mother raises her eyebrows, amused.

"Is that so? You know, Liam, Anna's not so bad at the violin herself."

"I noticed," I mumble. All the blood in my body is in my face, and I'm feeling raw and caught out.

"Well, come on, Twyla. Let's go get a treat and leave these prodigies to go about their business." The dog whines slightly and snuffles after her to the kitchen.

I want to write more music, but we can hear Anna's mom opening cabinets and putting away groceries, and we both know the spell is broken. It's almost funny, the thunderous boom of making art giving way to the quiet, boring routines of daily life, and I smile at her as I gather my jacket and backpack.

"Maybe we should do this again sometime," I say. I mean it ironically, because at this point, I feel like we've been locked together by some powerful cosmic force.

She nods, though, with her characteristic gravity. "It's not just a song, Liam. I think it could be an entire show. Like a cross between a concert and a play."

As soon as she's spoken the words, I can see the entirety of it, lovely and fearsome in its perfection. I'm in a dream state while we say goodbye, Anna folding me in a hug that carries more feeling than your average celebration between artistic collaborators and then waving to me from the door while I back out of the driveway. She stays there as I pull away, the light from the house giving her a halo of light, like she herself is glowing. She is the sun, the center of a newly discovered world.

9

TO THE LEFT

I REFUSE MY FATHER'S offer to take me to the first rehearsal, opting to drive myself. A professional musician, after all, wouldn't rely on her father to chauffeur her around. But I am so terrified of getting stuck in traffic and arriving late that I race out of school and drive straight there, eating handfuls of pretzels instead of stopping for a real dinner, and I end up arriving tragically early instead. The rehearsal room isn't even unlocked yet, and I pace around the hallways of the empty university building for a few minutes before deciding to go wait on the front steps.

Elise called me the night before to wish me luck and, to her credit, she didn't give me a hard time about wanting to go to bed early instead of hanging out. "Look," Elise said, "you're like a thousand times better at violin than anyone I know. So don't let those snobs see you sweat, okay?"

It was not precisely the pep talk that I'd been hoping for, but as I shift to keep the material of my shirt from sticking to my moist armpits, I have to admit that Elise knows me. I wish she were here, actually, so I could tap into some of her effortless bravado. Instead, I sit alone and fight the urge to study my sheet music, pulling my school-issued *Of Mice and Men* out of my bag and pretending to be able to concentrate on what the words mean.

I can feel him approach and stand right in front of me, but I keep my head down, hoping I can avoid small talk. "Poor Lenny," the boy in front of me says.

He is also carrying a violin case. His sweater is a bit raggedy, and his thick brown hair looks like he forgot to comb it, but he has a confident, relaxed smile. I'm not sure whether to be charmed by his obvious ease or cowed by it.

"Poor rabbits," I say, trying to match the lightness in his tone.

"Junior-year English?" he says, nodding at the book, and I nod. "And you're new to state this year? Don't worry, we don't bite." It's such a clumsy way of demonstrating that he's a returning member that something comes over me and I make an honest-to-God joke.

"Too bad I do," I say, and then I wink, which makes him laugh.

Just then, Mr. Halloway walks up the steps, and he slaps the boy on the shoulder as he walks by. "There's our concertmaster," he says.

"Thanks, maestro," the boy says.

"You earned it. I'll let you enjoy it for a week before we start working on that concertino part in the Bartók." They laugh together, and I feel very small. Mr. Halloway turns to me.

"Anna, isn't it? We're glad to have you."

I muster a thank-you as he walks inside the building. Normally I would be overjoyed at this welcome from the conductor and the fact that he remembered my name. Now it's overshadowed by my nerves at meeting the first chair violin. No wonder his smile is so certain.

"Congratulations on being concertmaster," I say. "That's quite an accomplishment."

"No big deal," he says breezily. "I didn't catch your name. I'm Sergei. Like Rachmaninoff."

"I'm Anna," I say, shaking his hand and completely blanking on any famed musicians named Anna. My brain sticks at the curious Russian-ness of his name and I blurt out: "Like... Karenina, I guess?"

Sergei laughs and picks up his violin case. "Then I'm grateful there are no trains around here. I'll see you inside, Anna."

I pretend to read for a few more minutes, though concentration is even more hopeless than before. Really, I just let the words swarm in front of my eyes as I imagine my wrist skewered on a pitchfork, roasted over a fire, wrung to broken nothingness like the neck of a rabbit. I imagine it broken into tiny particles by the deafening sound waves of Liam's band. I let a few people with instrument cases walk past me and try to calibrate how many I have to let pass before the rehearsal room reaches a critical density. That level is essential to not having to interact with Sergei again before rehearsal begins. There's an arrogance to him that is both magnetic and aggressive, and if I think too much about it, I'll surely be too unnerved to play my best. And I have to play my best. This is it.

I make my way into the back of the room, where everyone is piling their coats and empty cases. I keep my hands gripped tight around my violin to stop them from shaking. I find my stand partner and introduce myself. Michelle is a freckled, athletic-looking senior with cool green eyes. She doesn't smile much.

"You care if we use my copy of the music?" Michelle asks. "I already have some fingerings marked." Then, without waiting for an answer, she turns around in her chair to continue talking to a friend who is seated behind us.

I wordlessly slide my own folder full of music under my chair and look around. I should be happy about my seat, which is right in the middle of the first violin section, but I can see Sergei joking with his stand partner a few rows ahead, and I can't help it: I want to be sitting there instead.

The first half of the rehearsal flies by. Mr. Halloway talks a little about the songs on the program for our first concert in only a few weeks, and we tentatively play through several of them. I'm buoyed by the sound, which already seems bigger and richer than that of the school orchestra. Then it's time to break into smaller groups for section work, and I trail Michelle and her friend to a classroom down the hall, wishing I didn't feel quite so much like a wayward puppy. The violin teacher, an elderly man with teeth that look too large for his face, grins at us from the front of the room.

"Later I'll let Sergei run these, but for tonight, let's all work through those tricky sections in the Dvořák," he says.

We play through some trouble spots, pencil in some bowings. At one point, he has us play one stand at a time. My nerves are pulled so tight that my fingers jerk like popcorn when Michelle and I play, but I manage to rein in the nervous energy and get through it. When we finish, the teacher points his bow at me and says, "Watch out for that one. She's a firecracker," and everyone laughs except for Michelle, who scowls. My wrist throbs, but I don't care. My fuse is lit; I'm ready to explode in a shower of spangled color.

When Sergei plays, I can tell he's the real deal. He's certainly not conventionally handsome, but something in the loose way he moves as he plays, the way he rolls his skinny body from side to side as though he simply can't help it, is very sexy, and my face gets hot as I watch him. Even so, he doesn't get called a firecracker.

We break rehearsal fifteen minutes early. Mr. Halloway has arranged for pizzas, a special treat for our first practice together and a saving grace for my growling stomach. "It's going to be a good season, folks," he says. My body is humming with so much excitement that I feel like a vibrating tuning fork, and despite my hunger, I wish that we would keep rehearsing for the full two hours; it would be a lot easier than trying to make small talk with a bunch of strangers, all of whom seem to have friends here already. I linger awkwardly around Michelle and her friend Daya for a few minutes while they ignore me, and then I fumble my way into a conversation about the latest Sandra Bullock movie with a threesome of viola players. They tolerate me, as I knew they would; viola players are always nicer than violinists. The pizza, at least, is excellent.

I am walking out to my car, the relief of getting through the evening making my chest feel like a newly unlatched birdcage, when I hear, "Hey! Anna Karenina!" from behind. Sergei is jogging toward me through the dim parking lot. A car honks and brakes to avoid him, and my hand involuntarily flies to my mouth at the close call, but he simply smiles and waves at the driver.

"Getting run over by a train is supposed to be my thing, remember?" I say as he comes close, panting.

He dismisses this with a wave of his hand. "It was a Geo Metro. It probably would have bounced off me." He smiles. "Where are you going now?"

"Oh," I say, getting a spidey-sense that he's about to ask me out, and caught between feelings of wanting that and not wanting it. "I have to drive back to Greenville. School in the morning. And my parents will stay up and wait for me," I add hurriedly. I'm talking too much, but I'm afraid to stop. "It being the first rehearsal and all."

"Right," he says, looking unperturbed by my dodge. "Come down early next week," he says. "We'll get some food." It's not a question, more like a sales pitch. I open my mouth, unsure yet what to say, unsure even what I think about the invitation, but Sergei takes it as a sign that I'm about to refuse and says, "Come on. Say yes."

And so...fuck it. I do.

"So you're saying he's not super hot, but would you describe him as specifically *not* hot?" Elise is flopped on the floor of her bedroom, pushing up periodically into a backbend and looking upside down at me. I am sitting in the desk chair like a normal person.

"What are you doing? Aren't we supposed to be leaving in five minutes?" I ask. It's Saturday, and I'm sleeping over at Elise's house. Elise has roped me into going to another concert, even though I would much, much rather be eating take-out Chinese food and falling asleep in front of a rented video. This concert, at least, is professional, a band called the

Nothings at a theater a forty-minute drive away. But we're carpooling with Liam and his bassist, Eric, and I'd prefer not to see either one of them ever again.

"Oh, they'll probably be fashionably late," Elise says, rolling up to her feet. "No need to be uptight about it. And why won't you tell me about your new boyfriend?"

"He's not my boyfriend," I say, and immediately hate how juvenile this sentence makes me sound. The truth is that it's hard for me to remember exactly what is so appealing about Sergei when I'm not in his presence. I can recall only his largish nose, his holey sweater, and the fact that I desire badly to be a better violinist than him. He's definitely one of those people who already seems like he's forty years old, and I can't tell if I like that about him or not. "He's not *not* hot," I say. "But I think it has mostly to do with his confidence or something."

"His *confidence*. Mmm, the way he rocks that violin," Elise says, laughing and grinding her hips as she searches through her closet for some wayward article of clothing. I hurl a balled-up sweatshirt at her head, even though what she said is kind of the truth.

"Elise! Liam's here!" her mother calls up the stairs.

"So much for fashionably late," I mutter not-so-under my breath.

"I still gotta do my hair," Elise says as she hops her way into a pair of tight black-and-white pants that I've never seen before. "Can you go talk to them?"

Of course. I groan and throw her a you-owe-me look, but the truth is that I can feel my irritation at Elise building, and I wouldn't mind a break from her before we spend the entire evening in each other's presence, so I check the contents of my purse and walk slowly to the kitchen, where I can hear the boys making small talk with Elise's mom.

"That's so great to hear about your band," she's saying. "Liam was always so musical. I remember him marching around this house in diapers, playing his little drum."

Liam smiles, runs his hand through his hair, somehow mussing it and making it look more perfect at the same time. "Thanks, Aunt Caroline. That's, um, really adding to my rock star persona," he says, and they both laugh. I bite my lip hard. It's not fair, really, when total jerks are so good-looking.

Eric laughs a beat late, a weird high-pitched laugh. He looks jumpy and is chewing a piece of gum so hard that I can hear the wet noises of his jaws as I approach. I'm aware that Elise has only engineered this outing so she will get to hang out with Eric, and I don't get it. Eric is strange and weaselly looking and has a sharp smell that I can't identify and is prone to long periods of staring into space. At least Sergei seems capable of holding up his end of a conversation.

"Anna," Elise's mom says, making room for me in their conversational circle. "How many outfits has Elise tried on so far?"

"Just one," I say. "She's been too busy doing gymnastics." Elise's mom rolls her eyes at this.

"How's state orchestra going?" Liam asks.

"Great," I say. I can feel a prickle of defensiveness even though this is a perfectly reasonable question, a surprisingly polite one, actually. "Everyone's so nice. And, you know, really talented."

"That's good," Liam says breezily. "I heard it was a real stab-you-in-the-back-so-I-can-get-your-seat situation. But I'm glad to hear everyone's as nice as you." He smiles at me, and Eric laughs again.

"Not everyone is as cutthroat as you, Liam," Elise's mom says as she gives me a sideways hug, but this only makes me feel worse, a shade more pathetic than I already was, and I'm relieved when she makes an exit. "I'll go see if I can hurry up Elise."

Eric and Liam start talking about a song they're working on while I wade through a flood of unbidden thoughts. I wish that Sergei looked more like Liam. Then I admit to myself that it's not only the way he looks—there's an expansive brightness to him that makes me feel like drawing close, taking shelter there. Then I feel irritated with myself and want to take it all back, and I envision Liam wrapping a microphone cord around the pain in my left hand and pulling, pulling, pulling, until it pops off.

"Let's go, bitches," Elise says, literally leaping into the room and doing a high rock-and-roll kick before playing air guitar and wriggling her back against a surprised-looking Eric. It is only seven o'clock, and I've already started wishing this evening was over.

10
TO THE RIGHT

IT'S BEEN SEVEN DAYS since Anna cracked the lock on a treasure chest of new musical possibility. Every time I hear the melody that she wrote about Elise playing in my head, I like it more, I like *her* more, and at the same time, I feel somehow worse. It takes me a few nights of stewing over it to figure out why, and when I do find the answer, it's a punch to the gut: If Anna's brave enough to mine her memories of Elise for this project, it means that I need to do the same with Julian. Anna and I are so, so different, but we both understand that deep, resonant shock of grief. I can feel that our parallel tragedies could give shape to a real piece of art, something rare and special. But even after all this time, the memories of Julian pulse with radioactive power, and it's hard to get too close.

I invite Anna to my writing spot in the park, but I ask her

to meet me there so I can steel myself on the drive over, build up a store of courage without having to talk to anyone, even her. She looks apprehensive as she gets out of her car. I still don't know exactly what I'm going to say. The wind tosses the trees, and Anna pulls her sweater more tightly around her.

"There's something I have to tell you," I say before I can chicken out. A look of deep sorrow passes over her features, and I realize she thinks I'm about to scuttle our project. "No," I say, rubbing my hands together to try to warm them up. It's really fall now. "About Julian."

"Oh," she says, sitting down heavily on a rock, looking not at all relieved. "Liam, you don't have to. Not if you don't want to."

"Yes I do." I sit down and fill my lungs with the cold air.

I have the strange sensation that I'm waiting to hear what comes out of my mouth in the same way Anna is. Later, I won't remember the exact words, because the memories are like water running out of a sieve, escaping in too many directions at once. I know that I tell her about Julian, about how they always had the air-conditioning turned up too high in the series of waiting rooms where I spent so much of my time. By then, I had become a connoisseur of waiting rooms—the excellent ones full of toys at the children's hospital an hour away from our house, the ones with the plush chairs and crisp magazines at the offices of various specialists, the one at the treatment center that was boring except for a nurse named Sharlene who kept a box of Transformers behind the desk just for me.

And then there was the last one, in a far corner of the local hospital. Of it, I can recall only the outsize chill and that the single vending machine had a bag of pretzels dangling precariously from its coil, and its nearness taunted me. My mom *always* brought my backpack with the books and crayons and fruit snacks and Mr. Peeps, but we'd left the house in a hurry and she'd forgotten. I waited there for the end of a night and most of a day with one parent, and then the other, as they alternated being with Julian. A couple times, for a few minutes, they both left, telling me to stay exactly where I was, which was something that had never happened before and which therefore scared the shit out of me. But most of the time, I just dozed on one of their laps, hibernating to keep myself warm, and I could feel the shiver in their chests sometimes, and I knew they were cold, too.

And then Aunt Caroline had come in the afternoon and picked me up, and I remember how shockingly warm her skin felt when she lifted me in her arms. "I'm sorry, little bug," she said into my hair, and I thought she was only apologizing for how long it took her to come get me. She drove me back to her house, back to Elise and David and Uncle Rick, and I have no memory of when the news came that Julian had died or who had been the one to deliver it to me.

I tell Anna about the cold waiting room, but that feels

false, I'm already doing this all wrong, because talking about Julian only in the moment of his death is something I loathe. The problem is that I don't have all that many specific memories of Julian, except a few when he yelled at me for playing with his toys or for being loud and annoying, and I know that isn't right to share either, because Julian was mostly kind to me, and the reason my memory sticks at his anger is because it was unusual. Instead, I try a different route. I share the slush of memories from when I would wake at night and feel cold, and I would sneak through the door to Julian's room. Our rooms were connected, really one large bedroom that a previous owner had divided at some point, but to slip into the half that wasn't mine felt like entering a different world. I would climb into bed next to Julian, warm myself with his heat, which radiated like a furnace. It was only much later that I realized his warmth stemmed from fevers that the treatments gave him; my own chill was from the air-conditioning that our parents turned up to keep him comfortable.

Julian usually slept heavily, and he wouldn't even move when I crawled into the bed and curved my body to fit next to him. Occasionally, though, he would wake up and smile drowsily at me and press his sweaty forehead against my cool one before slipping back into sleep. I wish that Julian had spoken to me in those moments, had told me stories or given me advice about how to survive in our stupid fucking family as an only child. But that, of course, was imagining Julian as the wise older brother, the way he would be now if he were still alive. In reality, he was only an eleven-year-old kid, and a scared and sheltered one at that.

I feel a drop in my stomach, and I'm bobsledding down a frozen track of memories now, both cold and hot: the ice chips that I liked feeding to Julian whenever he was in the hospital and the way that he would accept them every time, whether he was so sick he could barely move or felt just fine; the steaming cups of tea my mother used to make at night, so hot that they would sit on the counter for twenty or thirty minutes until they were cool enough to sip, and how I never see her drink tea anymore; the incredible stifling heat of the back seat of the car on a summer day and how Julian taught me to avoid the metal parts of the seat belt buckle; the class field trip to an ice rink in third grade and how I'd been inexplicably good at skating despite never having done it before, until Bryce Penske called me a fairy and then I avoided ice skating for years afterward without ever really stopping to remember why.

I'm here; I've landed at the bottom of the track, all those little fragments leading me here, and now I see what memory is waiting for me.

The summer I was thirteen, my parents rented a cottage on the lake for a whole month, the same as they'd done for several years prior. I always liked those summer vacations; I liked the way swimming for hours made me so hungry for grilled cheese sandwiches and the way my mother was so relaxed while reading in the lounge chair on the rocky beach and the way my father would simply disappear for days at a time while he tended to work matters at home. But that summer, discord was in the air. When it came to my parents, it was me versus them. They nagged; I complained. The smallest, most innocuous things—my haircut, the music I liked, the band T-shirts I bought with birthday money from Lolly and Gramps—became battlefields, and I retaliated with a battering ram of pure will that I pounded against anything my parents viewed favorably, including our time at the lake. I moodily stalked around the cottage, refusing to swim, complaining about the lack of a decent stereo, staying up late at night for no purpose other than to annoy my parents with the noise of the television and my rummaging through the kitchen.

It was at this already tense moment that I announced that I had no intention of joining the debate team the following year when I started high school, even though my father had been making passing references to it as though it was a foregone conclusion. I didn't understand my father's fierce love of debate. He claimed it was good training for law school, but from what I could tell, it bore little resemblance to anything my father did as an estate attorney, which seemed to consist mainly of shuffling endless reams of paper and meeting with crotchety old people. Besides, there was exactly a snowball's chance in hell that I would ever consider going to law school, and I marveled that my father had not already come to this conclusion on his own.

Nevertheless, that August afternoon when I mentioned I was planning on trying out for the fall musical instead of debate team, my father gritted his teeth so hard that he looked like he might crack a molar.

"This is about me, I guess," he said. "You would do anything rather than follow my advice, even if it means destroying your own college application."

I did not yet possess the argumentative poise to explain to him that his insistence on making everything about himself was a sign of extreme egomania and a distinct disinterest in my own personality and strengths. (I would learn to point this out often about a year later, without the aid of debate team training.) Instead, I said something eloquent like, "I don't care. You can't make me."

My father laughed bitterly. "I'm pretty sure I can make you. On the other hand, you could just choose to take my good advice. But you would fritter away any opportunity to spite me."

We were sitting on the screened-in back porch, which was a fraction cooler than the rest of the cottage. My mom was at the small table, not taking part in the conversation, but also not even pretending to work on the crossword she had started. My father was wearing pants even though it was over ninety, and I wondered how long it had been since I had seen his legs. Years, I was pretty sure.

"There's no reason you can't do both drama and debate if you learn some time management skills. You'll do debate this year or you won't do any extracurricular activities at all," he said.

"Fine, then I won't do anything," I said. "What about the college applications you're so fucking worried about?"

My father's jaw tightened again and for a second, I saw in him a desire to physically hurt me. Instead, he gripped the arm of the chair and said with feigned calm, "Don't use that kind of language with your mother and me." This made me roll my eyes, not only because of his stupidly prim argument but because my mother had nothing to do with this. I was about to say so, but then my father continued: "You have no respect for how hard we both work to give you the life you enjoy. You have no idea of what we went through to bring you into this world in the first place."

At this my mother put her pen down on the table with an audible *click*, but my father and I were too wrapped up in the fight to pay any attention.

"Anything wrong with your life, you try to blame on me. If you didn't want to be stuck with me, why'd you have me in the first place?"

There was something raw and ragged in the way my father sucked in his breath. "If you had any notion of what a disappointment you've been from the very start—"

"Don't," my mother said, and the one hard word was like a rock that crushed the rest of the sentence. My parents made eye contact, and I was momentarily baffled and paralyzed by the shame I saw on my father's face. It was the look of a person who had broken a promise or, at least, almost had.

I stood up and left the porch, my legs weak and my blood rushing in my ears even though I hadn't sorted out why yet. I could hear my mom snapping something angrily to him behind my back, something like, "You never get to take something like that back." I was unbearably hot all of a sudden, so for the first time that summer, I shed my clothes while walking and jumped off the small dock in my underwear. The water was surely warm enough for swimming because it was pretty shallow, but to me it felt icy, and my body began to shiver uncontrollably almost as soon as my head broke the surface of the water.

Julian. That was the word that she hadn't wanted him to say. I was sure of it. Why had I never considered the reason my parents waited so many years to have a second child or why, when they did, they chose the moment when their first child was fatally ill? Mom rarely talked about Julian's illness, but I could hear the practiced explanation of it that she gave when she had to: "We never found a bone marrow match, even though every member of the family was tested. We tried everything, literally everything." The fact that I'd been tested as an infant and proved to be not a match was not new information, but I'd always heard that last sentence as: *We tried*

100

every single treatment available, short of the bone marrow transplant that was out of our reach. And that was true. But now I understood the deeper truth of that statement, which was: *We even had a second child to try to produce a bone marrow match, but he turned out to be a fucking failure from the moment he entered the world.*

They'd never wanted me, which somehow made the fact that they didn't want me now so much worse. No wonder my father felt such deep resentment; not only had he ended up with an inferior replacement model for the child he'd actually wanted, but the knockoff hadn't even been a good source for parts.

I felt shocked, and worse, I felt stupid that I was shocked.

I treaded water for a long, long time out there, imagining myself a cold-water amoeba that would dry out and expire the second it crawled onto land. I stayed there long past the moment when I heard my father's car pull out of the driveway on the other side of the cottage, past when I heard voices carrying over the water, the sound of families being called in to dinner in the other houses that rimmed the lake's edge. Finally, my mother came out with a beach towel and sat on the end of the dock. I wanted to disappear, to slip under the surface of the water, but I was shivering and my arms and legs were rubbery with exhaustion, so I used the rickety old ladder to haul myself up beside her.

"You never wanted another kid." The words were like bile that I'd been holding in my mouth, and I couldn't help but spit them out.

She didn't say, "Of course I did!" or even reply directly to this charge, which I had to respect in its brash honesty.

"I love you more than you can know," she said instead while I was toweling the beads of water off my goose-bumped skin. "And your father does, too. It's just that he's been in pain for a decade, and he doesn't understand how to feel anything else." I didn't want to listen to my mom make apologies for my father, though, so I stumbled toward the cottage, picking up my discarded clothing as I went. My mother called my name once, but I ignored her. At what point had she realized that I wasn't going to be anybody's savior? My first day of life? Before that? She must have wanted to get rid of me. Instead, she embarked on a lifelong ruse, playing out the charade of our having a normal parent-child relationship. I wanted to throw up, wished I could physically expel the bad feeling from my body, but I didn't feel nauseous, only exhausted. I collapsed onto the bed in my room.

When I woke up, I was sweating from the quilt that my mother had put over me. I'd slept straight through to the next morning, and while I was unconscious, my mother had walked all the way into town to get doughnuts from the little bakery she liked, and she'd left several on the counter for me with a note: *Having you turned out to be one of the best decisions of my life.* Standing by the window, I could see the blond glint of her hair from where she was sitting in her lounge chair out back, and I decided then that I would accept her lie, accept her peace offering, because I had no other choice. My father was a different matter altogether. I'd make it to eighteen, I resolved, and then I'd never speak to him again.

I cried then, choking, ugly, snotty tears that overwhelmed me like a powerful swell, and then stopped just as abruptly. I ate a jelly doughnut. I realized that I smelled of body odor and lake funk, and so I took a shower, long and hot, and when I got out, life kept going. I didn't talk about my brother again with my parents for months or maybe even years, but my father didn't say a single goddamn word when I didn't sign up for debate team that fall.

To be honest, I'm not completely sure if these stories have made any sense to Anna or even if all the words have made it past my throat and been uttered out loud. I haven't been able to look directly at her since I began speaking, and I've been running on and on for what now seems like an embarrassingly long time. I finally look her in the face, terrified that I'll see pity there. Instead, there's an expression that's difficult to read. It lies somewhere between solemn and angry, and I'm thrown off by its ferocity.

She doesn't say anything, and I'm finding it difficult to swallow, my mouth pooling with my own saliva. But then she stands up and gets her violin out of the case and starts to play, and the sound is so lovely, like I've been waiting my whole life to hear these notes. She plays the same melody we've been working on, but it soon branches off in a new direction, slow and sad notes, but with phrases that resolve themselves sweetly, almost brightly.

I feel like singing, so I do: "A blood cell, the spinning globe, a universe beyond our reach. Is it ever this cold in the marrow of the world?"

Anna ends on a final haunting phrase and lets it echo across the landscape. "Yes," she says, nodding, because that's all there is left to say. If anyone else was here, they'd see two people quietly making music, but for me, it's as explosive as a bomb going off.

She sits down next to me, so close that when we lean our shoulders together, it feels as though we are holding each other up. With her head bowed so close to me, I can see the neat part in her hair, I can smell her shampoo, just like at Elise's funeral, something floral. Jasmine, maybe? I feel shaky, but all the noise in my head gets swept away by the relief of not having to hold that memory all to myself anymore.

We walk to our cars, and I realize that I could reach out now and kiss her. It would be easy, effortless. We're attracted to each other, and it's what we're both expecting; I know that.

But now there's a stuttering, panicky feeling in my chest, and it keeps me from closing the distance between us. There's no mom to get in the way this time, not even the center console of a car to get in the way. But I've risked so much to tell her this particular story; I can't let it get swallowed by all the sinkholes of being someone's boyfriend. Especially someone who reminds me constantly of my dead cousin. And now she's tangled up with my memories of Julian. And Jesus, I couldn't even make things work with Muriel, who was basically my mirror image. How could I ever have a decent relationship with Anna, who is so, so different from me? I am the meteor bent on collision; she, the unsuspecting planet. It will be a disaster, surely, and Anna is not the sort of person who deserves that.

I hate when I get like this, so much noise in my head, all of it souring the sweet relief I felt leaning against her only minutes before. I want to exist in the moment, but I can't; there's too much static from the past and the future scrambling my brain.

She's only a few inches away from me, and it occurs to me that she might be the one to reach out and kiss me, so I do some fancy footwork, making a show of opening her car door for her, but also putting some space between us. "Your carriage, madame," I say.

"Thanks," she says, smiling, though her mouth looks a little tight, taking a beat too long before she gets into her car. "Well, good night." She is confused by me, as most normal people are. She won't wait around for me forever.

It's only when I'm standing alone in the parking lot that I wonder if I'm making decisions about Anna to avoid one more failure or punishing myself for all the ones that have come before.

11

TO THE LEFT

WHY ARE THE SIMPLEST things so hard for me? Trying to figure out what to do with my hands at the show is like trying to land a rocket on the moon. I can't dance like Elise, and folding my arms makes me feel like a security guard in the middle of a party. I should have worn pants with pockets, but instead I went with a red-and-black skirt that once again feels all wrong.

Liam studies me for a moment, and I try to convince myself that he's reflexively checking me out until he asks: "What are you doing? You look like a hall monitor."

I uncross my arms again and scowl at him. Elise and Eric have already danced away, squeezing through the crowd to get closer to the stage. Even from the back of the dance floor, I can sometimes see their skinny arms fly into the air. I reach again for pockets that aren't there, and Liam raises an eyebrow at me.

"I'm never sure what to do with my hands," I admit.

"Oh, Anna," Liam says, and walks away, leaving me there alone. So much for honesty. I stretch the fingers of my left hand back and try to pay attention to the band. They are, apparently, one of Eric's favorites, but it's hard for me to see the appeal. This is the third song, but I only know that because the crowd has periodically started clapping. Everything they play sounds exactly the same, and if someone told me that they have only one song that lasts ninety minutes, I'd believe it.

I use my time ignoring the music to zone out and rerun this week's rehearsal in my mind. I try to picture the entire room, to hear every measure of Dvořák's *New World Symphony*. My mind keeps floating back to Sergei, though. I've never met a Sergei before. Is he Russian? He doesn't have an accent. Maybe his parents are famous musicians who fled communist Russia before he was born. They play cello and French horn, I decide, and then I briefly imagine them playing some impossibly difficult song as my mother leaps around the stage at the apex of her career. They all take a curtain call together, not knowing that their children will someday dominate the violin scene as an unstoppable musical power couple.

"Here," Liam says, shoving a cup into my hand. "Sorry it took a while. There's a long line."

"What's this?" I ask, jostling back to reality.

"It's Coke," he says. "But really, it's just for the cup. It's for your hands."

Naturally. I'd been holding a drink at his show only a couple weeks ago. Sometimes I feel so awkward around people that I forget the simple solution. "That's really nice of you," I say.

"Well," he says, "it's sort of painful to watch you be so uncool."

We stand side by side for a few minutes, listening to the music and sipping at our cups with nothing to say to each other until Elise and Eric reappear and bowl into us, sweaty and sweatier.

"Isn't this fantastic?" Elise says while pinching my cheeks. I twist my face away from her fingers, spill cold soda down my shirt.

"Arr," I growl, but Elise ignores me. Eric is talking to Liam, bouncing up and down on the balls of his feet and mumbling things about the bass player.

"We're gonna go out to the parking lot so Eric can have a cigarette," Elise says. "Don't worry. I'll get my hand stamped and come right back."

"I'll come with you," I say, suddenly desperate not to be left alone with Liam.

Elise gives me a petulant look and leans in toward my ear to whisper-yell, "Be cool. I've almost trapped him in the sticky Venus flytrap of my sexiness."

"Ick," I say, but I stay dutifully in place as Elise flits off toward the exit with Eric. Now I'm left adrift in the vacuous, noodling sound of the band, afraid to dock myself too closely to Liam. I feel the need to say something, but my mind spins faster and faster with fewer and fewer words coming together, and I am intensely aware of the sweat of my armpits and the soda stain on my shirt.

Finally, Liam edges closer to me and says conspiratorially, "This band is pretty bad," and smiles in a way that seems almost friendly.

"Well," I say, "I think we can agree on that."

"I like them anyway," Liam says. "I used to listen to them a lot. Maybe five years ago? Anyway, I feel a connection to them even though I don't really listen to this kind of music anymore."

"You don't listen to bad music anymore?" I ask.

Liam laughs. "I mean, I don't listen to stupid stoner rock. It reminds me of being thirteen. To me, it sounds like a kid sulking at his parents' lake house. It sounds angry."

"As angry as the music you make with your band?" I mean this as a flip half joke, but he considers it seriously, for so many seconds that I wonder if maybe the conversation is over.

"Angrier, I think," he says, and because I have no idea how to respond to that, we go back to staring at the stage and sipping our drinks.

"What if we danced to this music the way people dance at your shows?" I say. "Like everyone can hear the angry?"

Liam laughs again, then throws up devil's horns and rocks forward and back repetitively. A little of his Coke sloshes out and onto the ankle of the man directly in front of us, and the man glances over his shoulder, annoyed. We lapse into silence once again.

This time the break in conversation makes me feel empty rather than merely awkward. There had been a connection between us that I've lost my hold on—a tiny chemical reaction that indicated that the space between us could be different—and then it vanished.

"Should we go find them?" Liam asks, and there's a distant politeness in his voice, and that makes me feel even worse than if he were being rude.

"Sure," I mumble. Liam tosses his nearly full drink into the trash on his way out the door, and I follow suit.

The parking lot is truly and deeply dark, juxtaposed with the nominally dark concert venue, and it takes a few seconds for my eyes to adjust. I briefly think about the fact that this is the sort of place where people are assaulted or kidnapped right before I trip on the uneven asphalt and collide with the ground. I catch myself on my left hand, and a wave of pain reverberates up my arm and rings in my head like a gong. No one is assaulting me but me.

I stupidly crouch there in the dark for a second, half expecting someone to help me up. But now I can see that Liam is already standing by the car, talking to Eric and Elise, and he doesn't sound happy. By the time I struggle to my feet and reach them, Eric is grinding something beneath the heel of his shoe, and the air smells like smoke, but not a kind of smoke that I recognize—not cigarette smoke or weed, but something with a fizzy, metallic edge.

"You're going to be totally worthless at rehearsal tomorrow," Liam says.

"What?" I ask. "What did I miss?"

Elise leaps up and bounces around me. "*Look*," she says, pointing across the street. "That's exactly what we need." It's a beaten-down bowling alley, the fluorescent sign flickering feebly above the door so that most of the time it reads OWL. Eric giggles and grabs Elise's hand and they take off running for the door, their arms waving like wild Muppets. I start to ask Liam what the hell is happening, but he's already following them, his hands shoved into his pockets and his shoulders hunched against the cold, and I have to scurry to keep up. Elise and Eric are already renting shoes when we find them.

"What size?" Eric asks me. "My treat."

"Um, my wrist hurts," I mutter. I bowl right-handed, but he doesn't have to know that.

"Suit yourself," Eric says, slapping a wad of crumpled bills on the counter. The cashier, a man with a very red face and a cowboy mustache, scowls and counts the money.

I take in the surroundings. This is a sad place. There are only four lanes, one of them closed because there's a big hole in it. Two of the lanes are hosting a league that is now wrapping up, and that section is awash in cigarette smoke and matching T-shirts. The carpet of the lobby looks like it hasn't been cleaned since before we were born. There's a ball polisher next to a gumball machine and a condom dispenser, but none of them seem to be functioning. Everywhere is the fog of almost, almost giving up.

"Elise," I say, but she is already headed to the empty lane, leaning into Eric as though they are lifelong friends, never so much as glancing back toward her actual lifelong friend. *I could have broken my wrist in that parking lot, and she wouldn't even know it*, I think, even though the pain, admittedly, has already faded back to its usual level. For a few seconds I can't locate Liam, and the possibility that he has left us and is driving home alone flashes across my brain like lightning. But no, he's right over there, sitting on a stool near the closed lane and writing in a little notebook.

"Can't we knock them unconscious and drag them out of this place?" I ask, approaching him cautiously. Liam barely glances in my direction.

"Considered it," he says. "But Eric is sort of like a superhero when he's like this. He's impervious. Better to wait it out."

"When he's like what?"

"Super high on something or other."

"But what about Elise? She's your cousin." I feel a stab of

112

panic go through me. I knew Eric was no good. Why hadn't I told Elise that from the first moment we laid eyes on him?

"Elise makes her own decisions just like everyone else," Liam says. "It's not like anything I could say to her right now would matter anyway. Or anything you could say to her either."

There's a flare of anger, and all the reasons I can't stand Liam whoosh through me like the backdraft of a fire that has been hiding in the walls of my heart during the concert. What does he know about what I would say to Elise, or how those words would land with my best friend in the entire world? And beyond that, he is arrogant, he is self-centered, he is insufferable, his shoes look too big for his stupid feet, he probably spent hours in front of a mirror trying to get his hair to look so good, and...

"Look, you let things get to you too much. You know that, right?" Liam says this in a not-unkind tone of voice, but I'm not in the mood for anyone to tell me how I should or shouldn't be.

I turn on my heel, stomp away, and sink down uneasily onto one of the molded seats, all but invisible to the three of them as I wait for the world to spin us toward tomorrow.

"Smoldering Anna," Sergei says as we sit down in the tiny sandwich shop where we agreed to meet. The table is so small that my knees knock into his as I slide into the chair, but he doesn't adjust to make more room for me.

"Smoldering?" I say with a nervous laugh. "Hardly."

"It always looks like you're thinking about eighteen things at once," Sergei says, and then adds lightly, as though he's mentioning the time or the weather, "It's sexy." I'm at a loss for how to respond, so I take a deep drink of my water as soon as Sergei pours it for me. Yep, his real age should be calculated by a method similar to dog years—he's three times seventeen years at least. And yet, what's so wrong with maturity?

For a while, as we wait for our sandwiches to arrive, I ask him questions about the music we are playing in orchestra, probing gently for more information about the other people in the first violin section. It feels a little like I booked a business meeting with the concertmaster rather than agreed to a date. Sergei gamely tries to lighten the mood by telling a story about the time two years ago when Mr. Halloway started rehearsal with his fly unzipped and then had to dash into the hallway to fix it, and then returned to say, "Eighty-seven of you and not one of you could help a fellow out before he feels a breeze in the middle of Shostakovich?" This comment has become something of orchestra legend, according to Sergei, and is still broken out at key moments for comedic effect. I laugh at the story, though secretly I feel sorry for Mr. Halloway, who probably isn't paid enough to put up with all of us.

"All right," Sergei says as the sandwiches land on the

table. He has ordered tuna salad, the most loathsome choice imaginable, and I study my falafel closely to avoid watching him bite into it. "Enough about state sym. No more music talk for the rest of our date."

"Ah, yes, it must be so *tiresome* to be the best at something and have people want to *talk* to you about it," I mock, and he laughs and shrugs.

"Really, you're the only one who wants to talk to me about it," he says. "You're a little intense that way. Most of my friends at school do their best to ignore anything related to classical music, and my orchestra friends treat it as a dweeby secret of their own."

"Your family must be proud, though," I say, trying to wipe tahini sauce from my fingers. Why didn't I think to order something less messy? I steal a glance at him, happy that he is eating his pickle rather than the sandwich, and imagine again his exotic Russian-émigré parents, their treasured instruments smuggled to the US from under the veil of Soviet-era politics.

"Eh. Sure. I think my parents are mostly distracted by what to do with Reggie, my younger brother. He's a math prodigy, but also autistic, and he needs a lot of special teachers, and it takes up a lot of everyone's time. It's complicated."

I take a moment to absorb these facts—that his brother has such a non-Russian-sounding name, that Sergei is not the most remarkable one in his family. "Oh. I'm…sorry?" I say, but then feel my cheeks burn as though I've said something inappropriate. "What I mean is...it sounds like that could be hard for you."

Sergei taps his pickle on the plate, tilts his head to one side. I can see when he stretches his hand that he has the same weird curve in his left index finger as I do from too much practice—crooked violinist fingers. "Is it hard? Yes, I guess sometimes. Or more like, there are good and bad parts of being the person who is more okay, more capable of making decisions for himself."

"How do you mean?" I am a master of asking questions when I can hide behind them. It has long been my main conversational strategy.

"Well, you can sometimes do things without asking permission, and it goes unnoticed. I doubt my parents know where I am, and that's fine, because they know I can take care of myself, and I'll get back when I can. But then, being that person, the reliable one, can get a little lonely sometimes, too."

I swallow hard, knowing exactly what he means. A spot opens up in my chest for Sergei, a place I have been keeping closed off from him.

"I don't have any siblings," I say. "But I know what you mean about being the reliable one all the time."

"Yeah, maybe I guessed that about you," Sergei says, and he's smiling so warmly that I don't even mind that the air between us smells slightly of fish. "Is it your parents who are unreliable, or..."

"Oh, no, my parents are okay. I was talking about my friend Elise. She's like…a thunderstorm. Enjoyable, mostly, but you never know when the lightning is coming."

"Sounds anxiety-producing," Sergei says.

"Just frustrating, I guess. She's dating this new guy who is a drug addict. And I'm worried she's going to get too caught up in whatever he's doing." I know as I'm saying these words that they're not the full truth. To call Eric a drug addict after seeing him use drugs on a single night is an exaggeration. As for Elise, she was completely subdued when we woke up at her house the night after the concert. Her skin was an icky color of gray, and her eyes were swollen, and she groaned repeatedly that she felt ten times worse than that time she rode too many spinning rides at the county fair and puked corn dogs all over me. When I told her I wasn't about to sit around strange bowling alleys and watch her use drugs and that I didn't want to hang out with Eric again, Elise nodded, eyes wide, and said, "One hundred percent. I definitely don't want to feel like this again." And then we walked to the kitchen and pushed forkfuls of the pumpkin spice pancakes that Elise's mom had made around our plates, not saying much, and I had driven home thinking that maybe that was the end of it.

At the time, her words had flooded me with relief, but now, sitting here with Sergei, someone who clearly sees the world in more of an Anna way than an Elise way, I have an uneasy feeling that I can't quite trust what Elise said. I wonder, actually, whether I have ever been able to trust what Elise says.

"I've known her since we were so small," I say. "And it feels terrible to watch her make mistakes. But what can I do? Tattle to her parents like a second grader?"

"Yeah," Sergei says. "Maybe the thing to do is keep your distance for a while."

I feel a shock wave ripple through me as I glimpse an alternate reality without Elise. No petty little arguments, no tagging after Elise, no feeling like the back-seat driver of Elise's wild ride. But also, no late-night phone calls discussing whether Brian Larson or Jonathan Wiltmuller is the hottest guy in our grade, no laughing until my stomach muscles are sore at Elise's descriptions of wacky plans gone awry, no smelling the soft soapiness of Elise's hair when she launches herself like a cannonball into me and hugs me tight. It is unthinkable.

"But she's my best friend," I say weakly.

Sergei shrugs. "Sometimes friendships run their course. But what do I know? Don't listen to me." He smiles at me and then polishes off the black coffee he ordered with his sandwich. Elise and I go all the time to Higher Grounds, the coffee shop near our school, but we usually get lattes with amaretto syrup (me) or raspberry (Elise). No one our age drinks black coffee except, apparently, Sergei. He is putting his hand on mine now, as easily as if he were picking up a cup or spoon.

Our ugly violinists' hands, lying there on the table together. Maybe we are the same.

"But Anna," he says, "you don't have to be responsible for everyone's decisions."

Sergei picks up the check and when he's done at the cash register, we get in our respective cars to drive to rehearsal. I've lost track of time, and I swear when I see the clock in the car's dash. We arrive moments before Halloway pounds on the music stand with his baton, Sergei barely sliding into his chair in time to play the A note to which everyone tunes. For the entire first half of practice, my thoughts are a jumble—the fish on Sergei's breath, the thought of simply giving up Elise, the beautiful curve of Liam's jaw as he nodded to the music at the concert, Mr. Halloway's fly—and my wrist burns as my fingers fumble for the notes.

It is a relief, anyway, to be able to talk to Sergei and his friends during the break, to not feel like an insect clinging to the very edges of a conversation. Not much better, though, to be at the very center.

"This is Anna," Sergei announces to the circle of mostly nerdy-looking boys.

"Your name's a palindrome," says the gangly bass player.

"Are you using Sergei for his body?" the French horn player asks. He's only joking, but I don't know what to say.

"Actually, Anna hasn't decided yet if she wants to be my girlfriend," Sergei says, smiling slyly at me. "But she's going to have dinner with me next week anyway." I force myself to smile at him, knowing this, too, is only a kind of joke. A joke that is completely accurate.

It isn't until three days later, at my private lesson with Call-Me-Gary, that I realize the extent to which I have become an object of gossip. Mr. Foster tunes his violin at the top of our hour together, then tosses the swoop of honey-colored hair off his forehead (a habit that drives me crazy) and says, "So. I heard you and the first chair at state are now an item." He smiles at me as though proud of himself for knowing this.

"I, um, wouldn't say that exactly," I say, staring down at the pattern in the rug. "Who told you that anyway?"

"You wouldn't believe the rumor mill in this field, even at the amateur level," Mr. Foster says, waggling his bow at me. "Now, listen: Sometimes it's not a bad idea to, ah, *date upward* in a section. But falling for another musician is not for the faint of heart, Anna. Trust me. I learned that one the hard way." He shakes his weird hair out of his face again.

I refuse to ask him to elaborate, though he is obviously desperate to share more details. I busy myself pulling a book of études out of my case so he won't see me roll my eyes. What does he know anyway? Isn't every love affair its own story?

"Well," says Mr. Foster. "Don't say I didn't warn you."

How wonderful that we have met with a paradox.
Now we have some hope of making progress.

—NIELS BOHR, quantum physicist

12

TO THE RIGHT

WATCHING ANNA SIP HER latte as we wait for our names to be called, I appreciate anew her beautiful eyelashes, the way she blinks when she looks up at the ceiling, as though she can see something up there that no one else can.

Her gaze comes down, settles on me across the table.

"Nervous?" she breathes, barely a whisper.

"No," I say, and it's mostly true.

We're at a place called Higher Grounds. This is only a coffee shop to me, but to Anna, it's a place where she used to hang out with Elise, a place she admitted she's been avoiding since Elise's death. This is a small town, though, with only so many opportunities to perform, and it was Anna who found the flyer about the new open mic night here, who looked at me with shining eyes and said, "Let's do it."

Musically, we are more in sync than ever before. But ever since I stepped away from the edge of something romantic with Anna, something buried deep inside me feels like it's forever behind the beat. *She's like a bandmate*, I shamefully lie to myself. But let's be honest: I don't think about the smell of Gavin's hair; I don't close my eyes to better envision the shape of Eric's lips.

The crowd applauds tepidly for the slam poet right before us. When I see the actual tremble in Anna's hands as she fumbles with the buckles on her case, I want so badly to put my hand over hers, to steady her, to kiss her palms and tell her how magnificent she is. I'm thankful that we decided to try out only the lighter portions of the show tonight. We'll be doing the section that Anna calls the minuet: a dance between two people in triple time, an evolving circular structure that usually ends where it began. We envision it as a dance we're doing with Elise, or with the memory of her, at least. This isn't the part of the show when we talk about Elise's death. Even so, the nervous energy emanates from Anna like a wave.

My fears that she might fold under pressure are unfounded, though; Anna is an anxious sort, but I shouldn't forget that she's a performer, too, and she can grit her teeth and get it done when she needs to. We settle ourselves on the makeshift stage, and she takes a few preliminary runs up and down her fingerboard, the sound of her violin so wild and vibrant that the crowd goes quiet, even though she's only playing scales. That sound has become like nourishment I crave. She gives me a brisk nod.

I warm up the crowd for a minute, explaining as lightly as possible that we're writing a show about two people who were deeply important to us. Then it's time for Anna to begin playing, but before she does, she leans toward her microphone and says, "This is for Elise. I wish so badly that she were here tonight, and I know that, wherever she is, she wishes she could be here, too."

I feel a twinge of irritation tighten up my muscles. Anna hasn't mentioned that she's going to say this, and it feels a little cheap, a little bad-sort-of-sentimental. But there are plenty of people in this audience who knew Elise, or at least know what happened to her, so maybe Anna thought it would be strange not to offer some sort of opening statement. Anyway, Anna is playing now, and I force my attention back to the music.

We're using a cobbled-together series of loop pedals to record ourselves. I saw a band do this once at a show and loved the ingenuity of it, that it allows you to accompany yourself on the fly. After we started writing the show, I found a few old ones in two different secondhand instrument shops in Columbus and basically cleared my bank account buying them.

Now Anna plays the light, breezy motif that forms the backbone of the entire minuet. It sounds like a little kid waltzing around a living room—loose, dizzy, charming. She records herself, stops recording using one pedal, and then presses another pedal to play back the recording on a loop. Then, with the music playing in the background, she leans into the microphone and says, "When my friend Elise was seven years old, she decided to memorize every one of the colors in the Crayola sixty-four pack of crayons, and then, for some reason she never explained, decided to invent an ice cream flavor that went with every single one."

There's a murmur of quiet laughter in the crowd. They're interested. I can feel the spark. Now it's my turn to record. The song we've written is simply the names of all sixty-four crayon colors set to a melody that twines in and around Anna's violin track. I let the words rise gently from my chest like bubbles, so different from the punch-in-the-face vocals I have to muster when I perform with the band: "Lavender, red orange, indigo, brown." To be honest, these haven't been the easiest lyrics to memorize, so I close my eyes to focus, to get it right. I can feel the crowd looking at me, but more importantly, I can feel Anna looking at me, can feel those accumulating layers of song connecting us, pulling our centers toward each other. I get to the end of the melody without a hitch, ending on burnt sienna, and then manipulate the pedals to set it to repeat over the notes of the violin. When I look up at Anna, her face is alight with the joy of making music with me.

"She started with peach. The flavor she went with was…
peach," she says. Her delivery is good, and the audience laughs.
They get it; they feel it. "I wasn't there when she made peach
ice cream in the family ice cream maker, but rumor was that
she put in halved peaches out of a can, and they froze into
tooth-chipping rocks. Elise wasn't daunted. She moved on…
to mustard." She pauses for the laughter, then smiles. "It's
not what you think. It's worse." She looks down at the floor,
demure, but laughs along with them. "She had this idea that
lemon mixed with peanut butter would produce exactly the
right color. I was at her house that time, and I have to admit
that she was completely and totally right. That is not to say
that this batch was edible either."

The crowd is sliding into our pocket now, and I feel the
exhilaration of it swell in my chest. They are along for the
ride, and even if we were to lead them to much darker places,
they would follow. This is going to work.

"She abandoned the project soon after what we referred
to as the Lem-Nut Incident. But even now, when I'm working
at the ice cream shop, I see in Crayola colors. Did you know
that a vat of pistachio is the exact color of a sea green crayon
on a white piece of paper? Did you know that a bin of straw-
berry sauce is violet red but definitely not red violet? It's one
of the things Elise gave me—the language to see the world
in color."

We're off and running now. Anna plays a new melody

while I sing about swimming-pool blue, and we layer the track of her playing over the existing tracks. I tell a story about going to the pool as a kid with Julian and Elise and David, how we all ate Now and Later candy and stained our tongues a rainbow of colors.

We push forward, adding and subtracting musical tracks, telling a few more story fragments that circle around the theme of color. Anna talks about how she and Elise once took every hose and sprinkler from both of their houses to set up an "obstacle course of rainbows" in Elise's backyard. I sing about shimmering arcs of color; Anna throws in a little sample of "The Rainbow Connection." I talk about the time when Julian helped me melt down an entire box of crayons into a giant rainbow one, about how beautiful we thought it was and how our mother threw it out because it was so ugly that she thought it must have been an accident.

We're going way over the open mic time limit, but it doesn't matter. The audience is so still, so attentive. They're smiling, most of them rarely remembering to lift their coffee mugs to their lips. I can feel that this is it. This is the moment we will point to after we're both famous musicians with dozens of hits—the moment it all began.

Anna's on the last story now, and we've peeled back the musical layers until only that first lilting violin motif remains. She's talking about how she always wanted Elise to be more serious about playing the flute so they could be in the high school orchestra together, but how Elise got bored with it by the time they were in seventh grade. "Who wants to sit around reading sheet music?" Anna says, repeating Elise's words. "Who wants to take something as colorful as music and look at it in boring black and white?"

As Anna says the last line, she pushes the pedal and the music stops at exactly the right time, the silence like a held breath. We've been up here for less than fifteen minutes, but it feels like we've remade the world.

Then the applause begins, enthusiastic applause. Someone whistles from the back of the room. As we stand up and take small bows, the audience rises with us, giving us a standing ovation. I see a teary sheen of emotion in the eyes of the woman at the nearest table. Anna reaches over for my hand, and we take one more bow with our fingers intertwined. The crowd claps even louder. My mind strays again to the idea of kissing her; the show has gone without a hitch, exactly as I wanted, but instead of quelling my feelings for Anna, it has energized them, made them rise up in a swirling, staticky wave.

We slide back into our original seats, legs shaky like we've run a marathon. I can feel everyone's eyes still on us, long after we've left the stage, and there's a sort of pleasure in pretending like we don't notice, playing it cool while we sip our lattes and the next performer takes the stage.

As we're putting our coats on, getting ready to go, a man

approaches the table. He's short, balding, but carries himself as if he's the most important person in the room.

"I have to say, I was wowed by your performance tonight," he says, and before we can murmur our thanks, he thrusts his hand out for me to shake and says, "Ray Goodman. I manage the Greenville Playhouse. Do you have more?"

I know the Greenville Playhouse. It is a thoroughly local theater—I've gone there occasionally with my mom to see one of her friends in a play, and the die-hard musical theater nerds in my school are always rehearsing for something or other there. And yet, it's a real venue, not some coffee shop or pizza joint.

"More?" Anna says tentatively.

"More material," Ray says. "I have a one-week gap in our programming at the end of next month that I'm looking to fill. Could be a nice little piece, and without much production cost other than what you already have here. But you'd have to have, say, an hour of material to make it work."

"We have that already," I assure him smoothly. "We've been working on a full show for a couple months now, and it's coming together quickly." To say we have an hour of material is an exaggeration, but right now, anything feels possible. "We could definitely iron out the kinks by then."

Ray smiles at me, and I half expect him to say something old-timey like, "I like your style, kid." Instead, he says, "Look, guys, you should know that I can't pay you for this. The theater would keep the ticket sales. But I could make some flyers to distribute, print a few posters for outside the theater. And you could make a nice recording of the show from the theater's soundboard to use however you see fit. Sound all right?"

Anna is so flushed that I worry for a second she might do something embarrassing, like give Ray a hug. Instead, she takes my hand again and gives it a squeeze. "Yes," she says to Ray, though she never takes her eyes off mine. "That sounds all right."

My parents are still awake after I drop Anna off and drive home, and I tell them the news, though I gloss over what the subject matter of the show is. My mother hugs me and says, "It sounds great, Liam." Even my father's eyebrows raise a fraction of an inch, which might indicate that he is impressed.

I'm so tired that I almost drop into bed with my clothes still on, but the appeal of a hot shower is strong, and I stand in there for a while with my eyes closed, trying to figure out what's scratching at the very edges of my mind.

Then I remember the introduction Anna gave before the performance. But why is that a big deal? She was probably nervous, feeling the need to fill the air. It's more than that, though; it doesn't seem particularly true, what she said about Elise. *I wish so badly that she were here tonight, and I know that, wherever she is, she wishes she could be here, too.* For one, we wouldn't have written those songs if Elise were still around to hear them at an open mic, and for another, I think it's probably a mistake to assume that someone who drives head-on into oncoming traffic wants to be at a coffee shop or anywhere else. I don't have any interest in putting some warped version of my dead cousin on display.

But then—Julian is part of the show, too. What am I doing, thinking I can talk about Julian in any way that is truthful, when all I really have left of him are a handful of barely there impressions dredged up from the murk of early childhood?

I shut off the water and wipe the droplets from my face. I can find something wrong with anything, it seems, even creating art with a beautiful musician. It gets so tiring, being the one who's trapped in this head.

13

TO THE LEFT

LATELY, EVERY TIME I see Elise, I feel like I am tumbling to the bottom of a very deep pit. I somersault and twist on the way down, swinging wildly between trying to shut out the general state of things now and obsessing over every tiny detail—the furtive way she avoids ever mentioning Eric's name, the shadowy thumbprints under Elise's eyes, the way her skin seems thinner and blotchier, the strangely metallic smell to her sweat. I can't stop wondering if these are omens of some sinister, looming event.

Today, for instance, I should be practicing two new pieces for the winter concert, but as soon as I start playing, the idea of Elise keeps pressing at the corners of my brain, breaking my concentration, and after I mess up a simple section in the Strauss four times in a row, I give up and go over to Elise's house. I rarely turn up unexpectedly like this—that's usually Elise's job—but after letting me in with a slight raise of the eyebrows, Elise resumes scratching on a sketch pad at a feverish pace.

"Whatcha drawin'?" I ask, aiming for nonchalance.

"I'm developing a whole series of graphic novels about a teenage girl with one robotic eye that can see the future and one nonrobotic eye that's blind except for when there are evil spirits nearby."

I want to simply say, "Cool" (because honestly, it does sound kind of cool), but instead I hear myself saying, "Is this because Eric is into those Japanese cartoons?" I saw a patch sewn on his backpack, a cartoon girl with huge eyes, which I found weird and childish.

Elise gives me a nasty look. "No, it's because I'm an artistic genius."

"Okay," I say, silently vowing not to bring up Eric again. "How's your history project going?"

"Eh." Elise shrugs, not lifting her eyes from the paper. "Haven't started it yet."

"Elise!" I say. "It's due, like, tomorrow!"

Elise stops, shuffles through a few things in her backpack, crumpled papers that have fallen to the bottom. "No, here it is: essay on a piece of wartime propaganda. It's not due until Thursday." Elise flings the scrap in my direction and picks up her colored pencil again. She's right; it is, in fact, due the day after tomorrow, but it doesn't matter, because I've had it completed since last week. "Do you have something interesting to tell me, or did you just come over to play homework cop?"

I squirm, debating whether I should leave. I watch Elise while she draws. There's an oily clump of hair sticking up on one side of her head, like she hasn't washed it for a few days. "I think Sergei wants to have sex with me, but I'm not sure I want to," I blurt.

Elise's eyes flick up from the page. "Go on," she says, putting on a funny accent. I knew it would get her attention, even though it is, at best, a gross exaggeration. The truth is that I am never quite sure what Sergei wants from me, which is why dealing with him is so stressful. I've noticed that during rehearsal, he and the first chair cellist are always laughing together and sharing some sort of silent jokes across Mr. Halloway's conductor stand. This cellist has beautiful red hair and enormous boobs, and I'm not sure why he isn't trying to date her instead. Or maybe he already tried and failed?

"He keeps asking me to drive down on a weekend. Not for rehearsal, but just to hang out with him."

"Are you going to?" Elise asks. "Have sex with him, I mean?"

I shrug, indicating it's up in the air, though in truth it is impossible to imagine such a thing actually happening. Elise sighs and puts her pencil down, studies me for a moment.

"Let's watch *Little Women* and compare him to Laurie," she says, and I am flooded with such relief for this gift of normalcy that it takes all my willpower not to throw myself at Elise and cling to her.

I demur on a weekend trip down to see Sergei but, despite a lack of resemblance between him and Christian Bale, I do agree during a phone call to arrive early for rehearsal the next week so we can hang out. I expect him to give me directions to some restaurant again, but instead he tells me to go to a strip mall on the outskirts of the city.

"Also—and I'm not asking for any particular reason, of course—what's your favorite junk candy?"

"Um," I mutter, momentarily distracted by the notion that Sergei might be a serial killer trying to lure me to the middle of nowhere, "Dots, I guess?"

"Dots? *Dots?* What kind of choice is that? Dots. Good God. Well, don't be late and don't expect me to share my Kit-Kat," he says before hanging up.

When I arrive, Sergei is already standing in front of the bargain-run movie theater, a jumbo box of Dots and a king-sized KitKat in his hands. "Here," he says, tossing them to me. "Hide these in your bag."

"You trust me with this KitKat?" I deadpan, and then feel a charge of joy when he laughs at my joke.

"It's Classics Monday," he explains, and buys us two tickets to the showing of *Some Like It Hot* that's about to start.

"There's no way we have time to watch the whole thing," I protest, but Sergei only shrugs.

"An hour of Marilyn Monroe is better than no Marilyn at all, right?"

And he's right. The theater is sticky-floored and musty-smelling and I make myself queasy on a dinner of movie candy, but I have a good time, and I like hearing Sergei's goofy laugh when Jack Lemmon delivers a line. Sergei slips his arm around me, lets it rest comfortably on my shoulders, and doesn't try to feel me up or kiss me. It's enough to make me wonder why I've been feeling so divided when it comes to him.

We leave at the absolute last minute possible, and Sergei tells me to follow him in my car. But then I lose him when he slides through a yellow light, and I get turned around, and I have to stop at a sad-looking Citgo for directions. I'm sweating at this point and my heart is racing when I rush into rehearsal ten minutes late, and I can see Mr. Halloway glower as I hustle into my seat. He puts his baton down before we start a new piece and folds his arms.

"Folks, we have to get started at seven o'clock sharp if we're going to be ready for this concert," he says. "I will rearrange the section if some people don't think it's a priority to show up to rehearsal on time." He does not look at me when he says this, but I, along with everyone else, know he's referring only to me. My face feels like it's on fire.

When Halloway asks the cello section to play something, his back turned to the violins, Sergei turns around and mouths *Sorry* to me and pulls an apologetic frown. Instead of answering, I look down at the ground, still feeling like the breath is being squeezed out of me. My stand-mate Michelle gasps.

"Oh my God, do you have a thing with Master Igor?" she hisses, loud enough that her friend sitting in the row behind us starts to giggle. Halloway throws a nasty look over his shoulder.

"Let's get it together, people," he says.

I, however, cannot get it together. My hands are anxious but also too slow, sloppy and constantly behind the beat. The fast runs in the section of the Bartók we are practicing become inarticulate and slurred, and when I arrive at the resolving top note, a fraction of a second late, I can hear that it is out of tune. I missed tuning with the orchestra, so now I try to do it by softly, softly plucking the strings while Mr. Halloway is talking to the brass section.

"What is with you?" Michelle asks. "Too distracted by Master Igor's D to tune your D?"

Mr. Halloway puts his baton down on the stand in front of him and turns to face the first violins, his arms crossed. This time his eyes are fastened on mine.

"Anna, is there a problem?"

My tongue is a brick covered in sandpaper. "No, no. I'm just a little out of tune. Sorry."

He keeps staring at me. "Well, by all means, fix it," he says. "We've got nothing better to do. Sergei, play an A for Anna, please."

Sergei turns slightly and plays his A string that the entire orchestra is tuned to. I match it, then play chords to tune the other three strings. My hands are shaking on the pegs, my whole body is shaking, and Mr. Halloway and the other ninety people in the room are still staring at me. The E peg slips, and I have to stop to press it inward, but it feels like all the strength has drained from my arms and my wrist pain flares like an alarm. This feels like it has been going on for a year, even though, in reality, it is more like thirty seconds.

"Good?" Mr. Halloway says. I manage to nod, even though I am desperate for my body to break apart into separate particles and seep into the cracks in the floor, never to be seen again. Mr. Halloway mutters something that the first chair cellist smiles at, and then he begins rehearsing the brass section again.

"Stop that," Michelle snips, nodding at my knee, which is still jiggling in fear. I have to use my hand to make it stop, as though it is someone else's leg. Fuck Michelle anyway. Halloway never would have even noticed what I was doing if she hadn't opened her stupid mouth to comment on it. And why the hell was she using the name Igor to refer to Sergei?

It isn't until later in the rehearsal, when the adrenaline has mostly emptied from my veins, that I'm able to see it:

the way Sergei rounds his shoulders up over the violin when he's playing, the way his swaying back and forth makes him look like a hunchback with an unsteady walk. This makes me hate Michelle even more, and yet I can't help but wonder how many other people in the orchestra call him that. At the end of rehearsal, I practically throw my violin into the case and run to my car, desperate to avoid talking to anyone, especially Sergei.

The drive home is excruciating, the blur of the highway like a filmstrip that replays my humiliation over and over. I turn on the local pop radio station to try to drown out the echo of Mr. Halloway's voice in my brain, but instead of some upbeat danceable number, the Goo Goo Dolls are singing about how they don't want the world to see them, and it only amplifies my misery. My arm is a piece of hot taffy, melting, falling apart, unable to help my hand with the work of steering the car.

My dad is already in bed by the time I get home because he has to be at work by seven tomorrow, and my mom is alone on the couch, watching old footage of Twyla Tharp rehearsing. Uh-oh. Alarm bells. She's obviously having one of those I-could-have-been-a-contender, what-happened-to-the-life-I-had-planned kind of nights. I want desperately to slip by her and go to bed unnoticed, but there's no route to my bedroom that avoids her, and when she looks up at me and pats the spot on the couch beside her, I can see that there are tears in her eyes, so what else can I do?

My mom puts her arm around me and squeezes me too tight. "Wasn't she beautiful, Anna?"

Ugh. The truth is that it all looks so silly and dated to me: the shiny costumes, the big hair. But I know better than to say anything except "Yep."

"Almost four times your age, and she's still dancing today," she says. Usually when this happens, serving as silent witness to my mother's sadness is all that's required, but she's feeling talkative tonight. "You are so, so lucky, Anna," she says, "to be able to practice your art every day. Do you know how rare that is?"

This causes a bomb of nausea to go off in my stomach, and my throat is far too tight to say that nothing I'm doing feels rare or lucky these days. I look down at my mother's knee under the blanket, that offending part that broke so long before the rest of her body.

"My miracle," she says, running her fingertips through my hair. "You'll knock the world off its axis with your talent someday. You believe that, don't you?"

Twyla Tharp pounds her powerful feet into my melted-taffy wrist: lucky, lucky, lucky. I nod mutely in response to my mother's question and lay my head on her shoulder and close my eyes and let the sound of the television slide me into unconsciousness.

I'm not sure I can capture the tumult of the previous evening for Elise—I can already hear her saying, "You had to tune your violin in front of everyone? What's the big deal?"—so I've decided to say nothing at all. But this turns out to be an empty resolution, because Elise isn't at school. Her mysterious absence fills me with premature panic. Elise is one of those people who never gets sick, who never even gets a cold when everyone around her has one. When I think about where she might be, I come up completely blank, aside from a shifting cloud of anxiety at the center of which is Eric.

I cannot concentrate on anything, zoning out in English class, fiddling endlessly with the same geography worksheet. My left wrist burns, and the sensation is worse when I'm trying to take notes, even though that doesn't make any sense, my right hand being the one I write with. I imagine lying down next to a cold metal rail, and then a train thundering over my arm, pulverizing my Anna Karenina wrist. I imagine it being amputated in a Gothic lab-dungeon, then being affixed to a patchwork monster by a creepy, hunchbacked Igor.

"Earth to Anna," my history teacher, Mr. Carson, intones. I jump, and he says, "Ah, there. She's landed back among us, guys," as the class titters.

"I'm sorry, what?" I ask, feeling almost as hot all over as I did when Mr. Halloway had stared at me.

"I asked you if you know where Elise is," Mr. Carson says. He's a nice man, really, one of the older teachers who usually has an endless supply of goofy jokes and loud ties. "You two typically being inseparable and all."

"How should I know?" I say, pulling my arms in close. "I'm not in charge of Elise."

"Okay," Mr. Carson says, suddenly gentler. "Everybody, check to make sure your names are on your worksheets and pass them on up to the front." My eyes sting as I shuffle through the papers in my bag, but there's absolutely no way I will allow myself to openly cry at school, something I haven't done since the third grade, the day after my mother's other dog, Rudy, died of kidney failure. Tough little Rudy had been intensely loyal to me for no particular reason; he was always picking fights with the German shepherd next door whenever I was around, like he was a ten-pound knight defending my honor.

On my way out of the classroom, Mr. Carson says my name, and he's too close for me to ignore it. I turn and say, "I'm not responsible for everything Elise decides to do."

Mr. Carson sticks his hands up in an exaggerated I'm-innocent pose, but he says, "You're right. I was only going to say that whatever it is, the world will keep on turning, okay?"

I nod without looking at him and rush out of the building to my car. Poor Rudy, pissing all over the house. Not even my soft-hearted parents could bear the idea of paying for ongoing dialysis treatments on a miniature poodle. Twyla had whined next to his bed for weeks after he was gone. I imagine my decaying arm buried next to Rudy under the maple tree in the backyard, pushing up daisies. I drive past Elise's house, but her car isn't parked in the driveway.

Damn it, where is she?

I consider driving to Higher Grounds to see if she's there, but gnawing at my stomach is a queasy physical need to practice the new orchestra pieces. I have no choice but to be absolutely perfect next week at rehearsal. Anything less and I probably deserve to be relegated to the back of the section or maybe to be kicked out altogether.

I practice the Saint-Saëns first, which is the one I like better. I intend to use it as a pick-me-up, but today it sounds too wooden and heavy, none of the pop and spring that I know it should have. I grip the body of the violin, torquing my wrist around to reach for the high notes, and the pain shoots all the way down to my elbow. It does sound a little better, though. Again, again, again. Every time I want to stop to rest, I recall Mr. Halloway giving me that hard stare.

I'm starting to work on the Bartók, which is a slog on the best of days, when I hear the front door open and close and wonder why my mom is home early, but I don't have time to stop and ask her. A moment later the door to my room bursts open, and my heart stops for a second as Elise shouts, "Boo!" and then collapses onto the floor, giggling.

"Geez, Elise, you almost gave me a heart attack," I say.

This makes me sound so much like a pearl-clutching grandmother that I try for indifference when I ask: "Where were you today, anyway?"

Elise stretches slowly, wallowing on the carpet like a cat, and says, "Helping the Hummels, who are sick with scarlet fever."

It's a sign of how turbulent the past twenty-four hours of my life have been that it takes me several beats of confusion before I recognize this as a *Little Women* joke. There is something not quite right about Elise, but it's not at all like the frenetic, constant motion of the Elise at the bowling alley. In fact, it's sort of the opposite, as though she's acquired a slo-mo setting.

"Gotta watch those babies with scarlet fever," I reply lamely. "They'll get you every time."

"I know, riiiiiight?" Elise says, giggling again and then yawning.

"Seriously, Elise, where were you? Everyone was asking about you today."

Elise pushes herself up on her elbows. "I'll tell you, but you have to promise not to get all judgy and weird. It was a one-time thing." I feel a little ill at whatever Eric-laced revelation is coming, but I nod. "I went on a hike with Eric. That's all." I have never known Elise to be a particular fan of hiking. "And then he mixed us some cough syrup cocktails when we got back to his car, just so we could relax and enjoy the sunshine."

"Elise," I say, all of the admonitions tangled on the tip of my tongue. "What will happen when the school calls your house about the absence?"

"Pffft," Elise says, waving this question out of the air like a bothersome fly. "I'm not an idiot. I went home and erased the message from the answering machine before I came here. And I'll forge a note tomorrow to get it excused." She seems to momentarily drift away. "The sunlight on the trees, Anna, was the most perfect thing."

"Elise," I say again, loading the word with all the judgments I have promised to withhold.

"Anna," Elise says, matching my tone. Then she reaches over and tugs on the bottom of my jeans. "It's just one day, okay?"

And what can I do, really? I could yell or cry or say I am worried, I could threaten to tell Elise's parents, but what would it change? The only effect is that it would activate Elise's wrath and possibly make her even harder to keep track of.

"You don't care if I take a nap here before I drive home, do you, Anna banana?" Elise says. "Don't worry; the violin music won't bother me." She is asleep almost before she has finished the sentence, leaving me to practice Richard Strauss's *Tod und Verklärung* over the sound of her quiet snores.

14

TO THE RIGHT

ANNA IS LIKE A twittering bird at our next rehearsal, alighting on a dozen different branches of ideas. "I feel like my head hasn't stopped spinning since we performed on Friday." She beams her most radiant smile at me. "It was great, wasn't it?"

"You're right," I say, though her exuberance only makes me feel anxious. "It felt great."

She picks up her violin and runs a few arpeggios to warm up her fingers. Then she starts to play a tune that is as lovely as all the songs she plays. Her tone is so beautiful, the deep rich undertones always there beneath the soprano violin notes, like the shape of her body under her clothes. I try to feel what an audience would feel, listening to it for the first time. They would be impressed. But I can't help it; I know that the same moment that set Anna's ideas racing has bumped me into the bleak landscape of second guesses. What if we hadn't decided to play at the open mic? Am I happier in the version of the world where we never started mining our tragedies for material? But I'm sure that I'll never be able to explain such lame feelings to Anna, who has finished playing and is turning her wide eyes toward me.

"It's really good," I say, because it is. The compliment turns her cheeks pink.

"Thanks," she says. "I'll record it for you so you can work on the words. I feel like we should put a little echo of it in the other section I mentioned, the part where you and I meet for the first time."

This again. "You mean when we're kids? You know I don't remember that, not that well."

"I know," she says, and I wait a beat for her to say more, but she's pressing her lips together, expressly not saying something.

"Does that offend you? I was like nine years old."

"You were ten, I think. And no, I'm not offended. It's weird, though, because I remember it so vividly. But maybe there's a way to put it in the show anyway."

"Yeah, maybe." I look at her and feel acutely that she probably doesn't deserve to be sucked into my spiral of doubt, but it's already on my tongue. "Do you ever worry that we're not being totally honest? I'm thinking about Elise. I mean, the whole thing is supposed to be a kind of elegy to her, right?

But I worry that we're making her seem a lot simpler than she really was."

"What do you mean?"

The two of us stare at each other for a moment, blinking. It's not an aggressive standoff; I'm simply baffled that she is confused by what I said.

"I mean, she steered her car into an oncoming garbage truck. Does that seem like an uncomplicated personality to you?"

"Liam," Anna says, and her voice on this one word is small, like she is a child. Or maybe like the person she's talking to is. "It was an accident."

I look closely at her, realize that she is dead serious. I shake my head, sit down on Anna's parents' sofa, run my hands over my head. Do we simply see the world so differently that we read the same catastrophe as a completely different story? Or is she gaslighting me? I'm not sure which is worse, actually.

"She made a mistake, Liam," Anna is saying. "Elise was driving to work, and she misjudged how long she had to pass another car. That's what happened. It was a mistake."

"And you don't see how a mistake might be a product of one's mind? Or even one's subconscious?"

Anna looks startled. More than startled; she looks frightened, and I'm unsure if it's because of the truth I'm laying on her or the fact that I said those last few ideas a little louder than I meant to. Then I feel like a jerk, and I motion to her to sit down beside me.

"Look, it doesn't matter. It doesn't. The show is what matters." I am possibly saying this to convince myself as much as Anna, but regardless, she creeps over to me and sits down.

"Maybe we need to leave it alone for tonight," she says. "Artistic perspective. Come on, I'll take you out. I'll buy you a burrito at El Armadillo." I understand how much effort this requires, to take a step back from her relentless drive. I've never known anyone as hell-bent on success as she is. At least, except me.

"You told me you hate that place. It makes everyone gassy."

"Who cares?" she says, giving me a little push on the shoulder. "This show will be so good that even our farts will be works of musical genius."

And I can't help it: I laugh, and the feeling of faltering connection between the two of us is almost, almost swept away.

I drop Anna off after dinner and then drive straight to a muddy little pond I haven't been to for a while, not since I was dating Muriel and things were sort of okay between the two of us. It's not cold enough yet for the pond to be frozen over, but already there is a sheen of ice on the shallowest parts of the water's edge. Muriel liked this place because you can drive right up to it, and there was hardly ever anyone here. "The magic pond," she called it. I give myself a second to do something I almost never do, which is miss Muriel: the shine of her beautiful blond curls, the spot-on impressions she did of people we knew, the almost manic fun it could be to goof off with her on one of the good nights. In the dead of winter, we had once "ice skated" in our tennis shoes around the pond, a memory that is filled with hilarity and the squeal of Muriel's laughter, and it only occurs to me now that if we'd fallen through the ice, there would have been no one for miles around to help us. One weak spot in the ice, one wrong step…another world.

Muriel no longer goes to my school. She goes to some expensive private girls' school half an hour away. Muriel is what people my mom's age call "troubled." We stayed together for much longer than we should have, and we were always getting in fights, with Muriel crying and raging at the slightest of my actions. At the time, it was exhausting, but now I see that there was an advantage to dating someone who always seemed to be one step short of falling apart, which was that it was easy to pretend that none of our disagreements were my fault, that I only had to endure them until the moment when she tearfully apologized.

Being around Anna gives me none of those easy outs. Anna is as level-headed as they come, and it's hard to imagine her ever having a self-destructive thought. Maybe I'm too "troubled" for someone like her. Maybe I just want everyone to be more "troubled" than I am, even Elise.

And yet, I'm not wrong about the car wreck. I know I'm not. Elise and I shared blood, and in some ways, maybe I understand more of her than Anna can.

When I get home, I try to sit at the desk in my room, a place where I never work, and write down some ideas for lyrics, but it feels all wrong. I'm best when out in the world, when I'm operating on the fly—scribbling ideas while sitting on a boulder, hearing lyrics while driving, having ideas come to me while drifting through some stupid Advanced Chem assignment. It's one of the things I like about myself, that creating is simply part of me, but I sometimes wish I could be one of those people who can sit at a desk and force the ideas to come.

I'm saved from my own thoughts by the ring of the phone, and I know with absolute certainty that it's Anna, even before I pick up the old-fashioned rotary that I saved before my parents could throw it out.

"I was a jerk earlier," I admit without bothering to say hello.

"It's okay," Anna replies. "You were right. I can't know exactly what Elise was thinking. The day of the … wreck, but any other day, either."

"The show is good, Anna."

"I know it is. I'm not calling to have you remind me of that. I'm calling because I found something tonight that might help fix what you were talking about. Can you come over?"

"I thought you said we were taking a break for the evening." I secretly love this about her, that she can't turn off the creative impulse any more than I can, and I'm flooded with the warmth that comes with knowing you're not alone in the world.

"Like you weren't writing lyrics when I called?" she says. "Just come over, all right?"

"I'll be there soon."

She's in her pajamas when I get there, her hair still wet.

"Sorry," she says when she notices me looking at the happy ice-skating mice printed on her pants. "The solution came to me in the shower after you dropped me off."

"They're cute," I say, dwelling for a second too long on what they would feel like under my hands. "Are your parents home?"

"No," she says. "They're at…dance lessons? Film club? I don't know. Come in, though. I really have to show you something."

I follow her into the kitchen, where there's a very old cassette player sitting on the counter. "Whoa," I say. "Where'd you get this beauty?"

"I borrowed it from Mrs. Bernhardt next door," she says. "This is what I wanted you to hear." She puts an empty cassette case in my hand. It takes a beat for me to recognize that it's my handwriting on the paper insert: *ELA Productions*.

Anna hits play, and there's the click and whoosh of magnetic tape, conjuring a time far away.

"Next up, we have a musical treat for all you listeners out there. It's Liam with his newest single, 'Somewhere over the Pancakes.' So get out that maple syrup, ladies and germs, and take a bite out of this."

"What is this?" I murmur, transfixed by the recording. Then there it is, my own clear prepubescent voice, crooning a spoof of "Somewhere over the Rainbow," hamming it up with a bad Frank Sinatra impression. "Where butter melts like snowy flakes, away across the round pancakes, that's wherrrrre yoooooooou'll fiiiiiiiiind me."

"That's me on ukulele," Anna says, grinning.

"You're kidding," I say, but I know it's the truth. It must have been Elise doing that absurd introduction. "How much of this is there?"

"Over forty-five minutes," Anna says. "We were nothing if not ambitious. Do you remember making this?"

"Not at all," I say. Nevertheless, I understand that this is exactly the right thing for the show, an object to ground us, a real record of the past. And wasn't it better to have someone like Anna on your side, someone who worked to make things sharper, rather than someone like Muriel, who was forever blurring the simplest of interactions?

"You're thinking that if we use some pieces of it in the show..."

"...then the audience gets to actually hear Elise's voice, even if she's only ten. Better than relying on my sentimental version of her." I'm touched that she put so much thought into what I said, rather than writing me off as an asshole like most people probably would have. I feel the pressure of something inevitable squeezing my chest. Maybe she is the piece I've been missing. Just like this recording will complete the show, maybe she is exactly what I need to make me whole.

"It's perfect," I say, and I don't bother to explain that I'm not really talking about the cassette. She sits at the kitchen counter, traces small patterns with her beautiful fingers.

"I've been thinking about what you told me about Many Worlds," Anna says. I had no idea that she remembered that. "It's so hard to imagine a world in which I never met her. Without her, I'm not myself."

I lean against the counter, move my hand close to hers, press my fingertips against hers, forming a little tent or cave. "What about a world in which we never met?"

She smiles, stares at our hands. "A little easier to imagine, but I still don't want to."

Being someone's soulmate doesn't mean that they're like you. It means that they're your perfect counterpart, the harmony that rises up to meet the melody you didn't even know you were playing. When I'm touching her, I can feel and hear the whole of the symphony. I carefully pull my hand away from hers, and the movement makes her look up, into my eyes. I take the smooth curves of her face into my hands and, while the Elise of seven years ago performs a fake advertisement for toilet paper, I finally kiss her.

She pulls back for a moment, startled.

"You're sure?" she asks.

"More than I've been about anything in my life," I say, and she leans close again. For a moment I feel weightless, as if I am hurtling into the future. Her arms, her forehead, her nose—the remarkable closeness of another human body. The cassette player makes a clunking sound as that side of the tape comes to an end. Then there is only the feel of her lips on mine and that stillness that comes with the best kisses, that suspended silence as if we are beyond the earthly atmosphere, out where sound waves cannot travel.

15

TO THE LEFT

SERGEI CALLS MY HOUSE twice over the next three days, both times leaving messages with my mother, who passes them on with a raised eyebrow and suppressed questions. I do not want to discuss what happened at rehearsal, and I do not call him back, and when there are no more messages, I am relieved, as though one item has dropped off my list of things to worry about. Even so, it's a long list. Elise calls me right before I have to leave for a private violin lesson and asks me to drive her to one of Liam and Eric's band practices.

"I can't," I say. The truth is that even if I could, having to see Liam sounds like torture. He's been making more appearances in my dreams, dreams in which we are dancing effortlessly together at concerts, our bodies pressed together. I wake up sweaty, half aroused and one hundred percent embarrassed that I can't control my sleeping mind. "Why can't you drive yourself?"

"David's home for the weekend and needs the car," Elise pouts. "Just forget it." And then she hangs up on me.

I am consumed by thoughts of whether or not Elise made it to the rehearsal and if she's saying mean things about me to Liam. Even so, I do my best to focus during my lesson, because I've been practicing the orchestra music as though my life depends on it, and I can feel that Call-Me-Gary respects the extent to which I have lassoed the notes of the Bartók, pinned them to the ground with the strength of my will, my whole body.

"Nice work," he says. "Now you have to open the door to feeling it a little more."

"All I've been doing is feeling it," I mutter. Every time I play the final page of the piece, my left arm is like a cymbal crash of pain. I have learned how to seize onto it, ride it like a rope swing over a gaping ravine.

He frowns. "At some point, you have to begin pouring all your experiences, all those emotions from the rest of your life, into the music. Let's work on the Strauss."

I reluctantly shuffle through my sheet music. The Strauss piece is not nearly as technically demanding, and I wish we could spend our time working on the music I'm more worried about. But I am too dutiful to demand it.

"Strauss was a Romantic, particularly at this point in his career, all individuality and emotion. Sometimes I even think of a specific memory before I play this piece, try to draw that into the sound. Listen." Mr. Foster plays a minute or so of the piece. It's perfect. Of course it is; he's a professional. It's hard to scrape up emotion within me at this particular moment, aside from a measly envy I feel for Mr. Foster and his established career, but I am so consumed with trying that I don't notice the way he has sidled closer, crowding my personal space before he is even finished playing.

"Do you want to know what I was thinking about?" he asks, his smile looking weirdly self-pleased.

"No," I say, a little too loud. And then: "I mean, I have to use my own memories, not yours."

He shrugs, gives me that smirk again. "Fair enough. You try."

My arm hurts. My head hurts. I don't want to be here. I don't want him to watch me while I play. I do it anyway, and even I can hear how anxious the notes sound. He edges closer still while I'm playing, until my arm is almost brushing against him, and when I am finished, Call-Me-Gary shakes his head, and I detect a little pity in the movement, which makes me want to scream.

"You're so tightly wound, Anna," he says. He puts his hand on the back of my neck, squeezing it like I'm a kitten he's picking up by its scruff. I can hear him breathing in and out. "You'd be a better violinist if you learned to relax a little." He's too close, so close that if I turn my head, I won't be able to avoid my lips touching his.

"I have to go," I say, quickly stepping sideways, away from him. He smiles at me as if to say that this disappointing response is all he could have anticipated from me.

I pack up my violin and sheet music and walk out of the house without bothering to say goodbye to Call-Me-Gary. I throw my case in the back seat and start the car in a hurry, eager to be away from this place. Gross. I glance in the rearview mirror, half expecting him to be smirking at me from a window, but there's nothing but the bland exterior of Mr. Foster's mother's house. Had I imagined him crossing a line? I hadn't. I've never liked him, and now it seems absurd that I never before understood exactly why. I'm not going back there. I will have to figure out the state orchestra pieces myself from now on, because I am never going to another private lesson with him, and it's this thought, on top of everything else, that makes my eyes go watery. I am so, so tired.

I drive past Elise's house and consider stopping to unload what just happened, but then remember she's probably off with Eric and Liam. Shaky exhaustion gives rise to a single thought that repeats and repeats in my head: Why isn't there anyone in this world who can make life easier for me? Why does everyone else only make life harder?

I go home to practice more. I won't let Call-Me-Gary take this away from me. I won't. All the orchestra passages that had sounded under control a few hours ago, though, now sound as if they've been sent skittering on a thin sheet of ice.

I don't get a call from Sergei asking me to come early to the city before rehearsal, and I prepare myself with an armor of indifference. But when I pull into the parking lot (twenty minutes early, determined to avoid any possible reason I might draw Mr. Halloway's negative attention), Sergei is already there, parked in the same part of the lot where I always park, leaning against his car like he's expecting me. He's wearing that same ratty sweater he was wearing when we first met. His hair hasn't been trimmed for a while, and because it's so perfectly straight, it gives him the look of one of those long-haired rabbits.

"Hey," he says before I'm even fully out of the car. "Sorry about last week."

"Why'd you ditch me like that?" I ask. I hadn't been planning to ask this question, and I hate that my voice carries a hurt edge.

His eyes widen. "You think I did that on purpose? I wasn't paying attention, and then I lost you behind a line of cars. That's all." He squeezes me in a half hug, but I go stiff, making the gesture even more awkward.

I shake my head, push him away. "Mr. Halloway hates me now. So thanks for that."

"Aw, Anna, he was just being grouchy last week. He's probably completely forgotten about it."

"That's easy for you to say, Sergei." I turn my back on him to get my violin case out of the car. "You'll feel bad about it when you're still sitting in first chair and I'm booted out of the orchestra."

"Oh, come on," he says. Over the past few weeks, he's been pursuing me in a puppyish way, cheerful and unflagging. Now, for the first time, I see a look of annoyance pass over his features, and it hurts me despite everything else. "Don't be like that. You're always acting as though everyone's out to get you. That's not the way the world is."

I am drawing breath to tell him that that is *exactly* the way the world is, but then I hear my name being called from across the parking lot.

"Is that Anna over there?" the voice is saying. "Harsh critic of rock concerts and bowling alleys everywhere?" I peer into the gloom of the dim lot to pick out his silhouette, but I already recognize the voice. I realize, with a sinking feeling, that my heart is beating hard and fast, and it's not because I've been arguing with Sergei.

"Liam," I say as he walks closer. "What are you doing here?"

"The choir's here for the first half of rehearsal tonight to practice those two overlapping numbers for the winter concert," Sergei informs me. "Halloway announced it last week." I must have been too distracted then to absorb these facts.

There's a pause and then Sergei and Liam introduce themselves to each other. I suppose that I should have been the one to do this, but I felt too flustered to manage it.

"I thought you weren't going to do state this year," I say. "I thought the drive down here was too much trouble."

Liam shrugs. "I was going to quit, but then they promised me I could have the solo from *Pagliacci*." When Sergei and I say nothing about this, he adds, "You know, the one where he's sitting in front of the mirror about to kill his wife and—"

"I know what 'Vesti la giubba' is about," Sergei says. "We've been rehearsing it for weeks."

There's another awkward lull and then Liam starts to excuse himself to go inside and warm up.

"No, wait," I say, catching at his coat sleeve. "I need to talk to him for a minute," I tell Sergei.

He spreads his fingers in the air as if to say, "Be my guest," then shoulders his violin case and walks toward the building. He glances over his shoulder and says, "Don't be late, though." He's smiling, but there's a little acid in it.

"I get the feeling he thinks a lot of himself," Liam says as we watch Sergei recede.

I can't help it; that makes me snort. "An interesting observation, coming from you."

Liam is wearing that cocky half smile that he uses to excess, but I can't help being attracted to it anyway. "Look, were you just using me as an excuse to get away from Stradivarius?" he asks. "'Cause that's fine, but I've got stuff to do."

"No, no," I say. "Sergei is…never mind. I wanted to ask you about Elise. Did you know that she and Eric cut school the other day to drink cough syrup?"

Liam tilts his head slightly, signaling his bafflement. "How would I know something like that?"

I almost answer that question earnestly, almost tell him that real friends, real human beings, share their lives with each other, so it wasn't so out of the question that Eric might tell him about the fact that he's currently ruining his cousin's life. But then I recognize that his was not an actual question, but, like so much of what he says, a way of showing me that I am tragically uncool for caring about the things I care about. Instead, I say: "I love Elise. I don't want her to make the kind of mistake that's so big she can't get away from it, you know?"

Liam nods in a way that is vaguely conciliatory. "I know you and Elise are tight. I know you want to protect her. But really, what can you do here? Dictate how she spends her time? Explain to Eric that drugs are bad? I mean, Anna…" He shrugs. "There's only so much you can do about how other people choose to act."

This has echoes of the philosophical tone that Sergei has taken with me moments before, of the worldly advice that

Call-Me-Gary doled out right before he pawed at me, and it kindles deep within me a clawing rage. I am so sick of people, of men, acting as though they are all-seeing sages while I am some kind of idiot in the matters of my own life. Do they understand how hard I am trying all the time? I shoulder past Liam, giving him a shove sideways with my violin case. I will solve everything myself, because solving things myself is what I always do.

"Damn, Anna, you practically took off my arm," Liam yells after me. "Better be glad I'm not your violinist boyfriend, or I'd accuse you of musical sabotage."

I spin back toward him, breathing hard. "He's not my boyfriend" is what comes out of my mouth, and I wonder at what point, if any, I will stop insisting that Sergei is not my boyfriend.

"Better not tell him that," Liam says, and then he laughs, and I can't think of anything intelligent to say, so I turn away again and stomp toward the door. I arrive at the building at the exact same time as Michelle and one of her friends. Great. Things keep getting better.

"Aaaaanna," Michelle coos as they trail me to the rehearsal room. "Who's that hottie you were yelling at in the parking lot?"

"Nobody," I hiss.

"Told you she was a mysterious little slut," Michelle says in a stage whisper to her friend, and they both giggle loudly.

I only make it through the first half of rehearsal by

refusing to look in the direction of Liam and the other soloists. It's not an easy task since they're standing right next to Mr. Halloway, but I'm worried that if I look at his confident smirk, at the angular shoulders under his sweater, at the strong hands holding his sheet music, my heart will begin to audibly thunder, my face will flush, it will be harder to pretend to myself that I don't have a crush on him and harder to accept how stupid it is that I do. After everything, I still do. It doesn't help that he sings so beautifully that Mr. Halloway says, "Great, just gorgeous," when he's finished and leads the orchestra in a short round of applause for him. Out of the corner of my eye, I think I see Sergei and Liam shaking hands. Ugh. I might throw up.

I hide in the bathroom for the entirety of the mid-rehearsal break, thwarting any possibility that I will have to interact with Liam before he leaves. That, at least, I can control. I sit on the toilet, doubled over myself, my head resting on my knees, waiting for the minutes to tick by, trying to think of nothing at all.

I brace myself as I retake my seat, assuring myself that I can zone out and coast through the rest of practice as long as I don't make any mistakes that are too loud or obvious. My fortifications crumble, though, as Mr. Halloway makes the next announcement.

"All right, folks, I'm going to let our section leaders take the reins for the rest of the evening. Let's break out into groups to work out some of those trouble spots, okay?" Mr. Halloway looks at Sergei as he says this, and Sergei nods back at him as though he can't wait.

Even in the best of times, I don't particularly enjoy these section work groups. It feels degrading somehow, to be scrutinized and nitpicked by one's peers, and it carries none of the all-together-now, help-each-other-to-greater-heights vibe that the adults in the room seem to think it will. We drag our belongings to a smaller room and arrange our music stands in a circle, supposedly so we can talk more easily, but to me it feels as if we are about to be tossed into the center like a dogfight, unleashed two by two to tear at one another's necks with our teeth. Sergei adjusts the tension on his bow, smiles at everyone.

"Anybody have a spot that's giving them trouble?" he asks.

Most people avoid looking directly at him, shuffling their sheet music or studying their shoes. No one wants to be the first to announce their own shortcomings.

"How 'bout you, Ollie?" Sergei finally says, calling on his own stand-mate. This is the safe choice: boring, imperturbable Ollie is second chair, and the one least likely to lose face by playing something badly.

"I guess I'd say that high part in the Bartók," Ollie says blandly. It's a pretty obvious choice, since that part is impossible to play. It also happens to be the section that I was working on with Mr. Foster right before he descended into maximum creepitude, and I can't help but feel a wave of nausea go through me. I look at the clock above the door. We have literally been in this room for two minutes. That means there are about fifty-four more to go.

"Great choice!" Sergei says brightly. "Let's try playing that part as a group. Starting at the top of the last page."

We screech our way through it as a section, once, twice, thrice, but it isn't sounding any less like a group of angry cats. Sergei rubs his forehead. "It's sounding a little pitchy, guys," he says. For a second, I almost feel sorry for him; I wouldn't want to try to fix this. Then he says: "Let's play it stand by stand. Really try to listen to your partner, melt your sound together."

Sergei plays together with Ollie, and it sounds passable, even interesting, and it's obvious to everyone why they share the first stand. The quality of playing drops dramatically after this, however, and soon it's time for Michelle and me to play. I fold myself up and tuck myself away, playing softly, letting Michelle charge her way through, letting her offer up all her mistakes on a silver platter.

"Huh," Sergei says when we have finished. I expect him to talk to Michelle about all the notes that were excruciatingly out of tune, but instead he says, "Anna, where are you? It's like you disappeared."

We lock eyes, and I attempt to silently communicate to him to drop this, to leave it, to go on to the next stand, and if he does not, I will never snuggle next to him in a movie theater ever again. He says, "Come on, let's play it together, you and me." He tucks his violin under his chin. "Ready?"

I have been getting ready for this for an entire week or possibly forever. This music *will* do my bidding, even if the rest of the world won't. This time I play ferociously, loudly, too loudly, really, but it doesn't matter because Sergei can match it. My fingers pound down on the fingerboard, finding the right spots as if they are magnetically drawn there; my bow chases the notes out of the instrument. I am not so much melting together with Sergei as pushing him, snapping at him with the sound. My arm burns, and there's a muscle in my forearm that feels like it's a string stretched to the point of breaking, but I am committed now, I have sunk my fangs into the music, and they're stuck for good. We play together for a couple minutes tops, but we produce a sound that is about a million times more exciting than anything he could do with Ollie; I know this even before we stop and a few people start to murmur and tap their bows appreciatively on their stands. Michelle scowls at me.

Sergei shakes his hair out of his eyes. "I think I need a cigarette," he says, grinning, and everyone laughs except for Michelle and me. "That was singular, Anna," he says, and then turns to the next pair of violinists.

He seems pleased with himself, but I haven't managed to exorcise any of my angry demons with my playing, only conjured more. I envision ripping my left arm off at the elbow with only the strength of my right arm, seeing the blood splatter the white walls of the classroom, flinging it with superhuman power at Sergei's chest, giving everyone nightmares for weeks.

I burn like a flame through the rest of the section rehearsal and still feel hot as I put away my instrument and pull on my coat. Sergei dogs my steps out to the parking lot, where our cars are next to each other. I will not speak to him, even though he's chattering endlessly about stupid, inconsequential subjects: college basketball, a movie starring George Clooney.

As I am about to get into my car, Sergei grabs my sleeve and yanks on it. "You're the most complicated person I know," he says to me then, not as an accusation but as a simple fact, and then he kisses me lightly on the lips and gets into his own car. A moment before, I might have bitten him like a feral animal when he pressed his lips to mine, but now his statement only makes me feel exhausted and extinguished.

16

TO THE RIGHT

THERE'S SO MUCH TO do to get ready for the show over the next few weeks that the days rush by like a stream that's getting faster and faster. The school days are like rapids, something to be navigated and surpassed as efficiently as possible so I can get to rehearsals with Anna, which are now my reason for being. Every time I lay eyes on her, I think once again that love between musicians must be one of the most beautiful events the world can produce. Every moment between us over the past few weeks has been like a song, a composition that gets louder and more complex every time the cells of our bodies come into contact with one another.

"You're going over there again?" Chris gripes one day as we walk out to the senior parking lot after school. "Thursday used to be band practice day. Bros before hos, dude." It's the sort of thing that would have previously incensed me, that would have forced me to come up with some angry reply that would cause tension among the band members for days. Now I can't be bothered.

"Yeah, maybe after the show goes up," I say. "Let me know how practice goes." I close the car door like a punctuation mark, not bothering to glance at Chris's scowl as I back out of the space.

Even when Chris shouts after the car, "You're gonna kill the band!" I'm determined to let it roll right off my back.

Anna got the audiocassette digitized, and we've been playing around with the tracks, using snippets of Elise's radio patter, taking the silly song spoofs as jumping-off points for our own original melodies. Our creative energy never really flagged, but now that we're a couple, it's like the engine of it is running on jet fuel. When I wake up in the morning, Anna is the first thing I think of, her reedy voice humming a new melody as I drift back to consciousness, and at night, the lyrics that I've written that day are my lullaby.

I've even managed to come up with a little possible audio of Julian's voice, some sound I could take from home video footage of toddler Julian babbling his first sentences. In order to gain access to it, though, I have to explain way more about the show to my mom than I want to.

"I'm not getting up there and talking a lot about his death or our family or grief or any of it," I say, grateful I'm driving her to her book club when this comes up so that I don't have to look her in the eye. My mother doesn't say much for a couple minutes, and my mind has already ground forward, trying to fill the spaces in the show where I might have used the audio. But when I pull into the Dodsons' driveway, she surprises me.

"Of course you can use the tapes," she says. "There are several copies in the chest in my room." I know this already—that impossibly sad chest full of Julian's baby clothes and blankets, things that I never wore myself, maybe because my mother had sensed, even in my infancy, that Julian's things would need to be kept, remembered. "Whatever you want to say about Julian, I'm not going to stop you. You're his brother, and I don't have any interest in keeping the memory of him hostage." I can feel the "but" throbbing behind these statements, and I swallow hard, waiting for it. Here it comes. "But Liam, you should tell Dad what you're planning before the show opens. People don't like to be surprised by things like that."

The show has evolved far past the story that I told Anna that day at the park. I have no intention to talk onstage about what happened at the cottage; this isn't a show about my dad. And yet, even thinking about Julian when I'm in the same room as my father is usually enough to make me cringe.

"He'll freak out," I say.

"Maybe," she says. "But at least this way it won't be at your show." She pulls down the sun visor to fix her eye makeup in the mirror. "People are talking about the show, you know. One of the assistants at the office brought a flyer back from the diner across the street and asked me if it was you." This, more than anything, makes me want to jump out of my skin. The show is only three weeks away and we're still revising big chunks of it every day.

"Tell Anna I say hi," my mom says, getting out of the car. I invited Anna over to have dinner with my parents a couple weeks ago. The spaghetti and polite chitchat was awkward only in entirely expected ways ("Can you make a living playing the violin?" my father asked her, but as I cringed, Anna only replied gravely, "If you're good enough," and my father smiled as though he liked that answer). Since then, my mother has told me at least five times how much she likes Anna, how many nice things Aunt Caroline has to say about her. There always seems to be a thought missing at the end of these assertions, and I'm not certain if it's meant to be "...but she doesn't seem like your type," or "...so don't screw it up."

"I'll get a ride home with Linda," Mom says. "But really, Liam—tell your father about the show."

I know Mom is right. But when? How? We typically only see each other in the evenings, sometimes not even then because I've been rehearsing so much. And my father never asks me any questions about the show, so there are no doors to conversation magically opening between us.

I summon the courage one evening while my mother is working an open house, tell my father that I've been writing songs about memory, and my father nods blankly, but I can't make the word *Julian* come out of my mouth before the phone rings and my father disappears into his home office to take the call.

"Two more weeks, that's it," Anna says, putting her violin away. She wipes the resin from the strings and loosens the bow as though she is performing some thoughtless bodily necessity like brushing her teeth. "Can you believe it?"

The thought of opening night makes me a little queasy, but Anna looks so entirely happy that I hug her tight and kiss her instead of answering. We've decided to call the show *Ghost Melodies*, a name that Anna thinks is perfect but I am constantly second-guessing. I have such a hard time naming anything definitively. "How's your wrist feeling?" I ask.

"Great," says Anna. "Isn't that crazy? I mean, we're practicing all the time, maybe even more than when I was trying to get into state orchestra, but there's hardly any soreness. It's like every cell in my body knows how good this show is going to be."

As I'm about to leave Anna's house, eager to have a few minutes to think about something other than the show, her mom walks into the living room, looking triumphant.

"Guess what?" she says.

And Anna says, "The interview?" and gives a squeal of delight when her mom nods. I don't connect this to having anything to do with me until Anna turns and squeezes my hands so tightly that it feels like she might be attempting to permanently maim me. "My mom contacted Cassandra St. Claire at the newspaper. She's going to write an article about the show!"

"She's a friend of a friend," her mom says, shrugging, though she's clearly pleased with herself for pulling this off. "She wants to talk to you guys next week." Then she starts humming to herself and exits the room with a lilting step.

"Our little show is making its way into the big world," Anna says. "This is going to change everything." I would like to say something meaningful in response, but I'm having a hard time ignoring the dark rumbles of a coming storm that thunder through my chest.

Anna's car is parked at Higher Grounds. She's obviously been waiting for me and is standing outside my car before I've put it in park. I can tell how deeply anxious she is, so before I get out of the car, I take her hand and say, "This is when we fly." The smile she gives me is so sweet, so perfect, that it makes me want to be this version of myself all the time.

The reporter who will be interviewing us is already seated

at a table drinking one of the largest cappuccinos I've ever seen. She has wild gray-blond curls and wears deep red lipstick. "There they are, the talk of the town!" she booms, followed by a smoker's laugh, when she sees us approaching. Cassandra St. Claire is something of a town celebrity, being the one and only culture critic.

"Get yourself something to drink," she says. "It's on the *News Journal* as long as it's a small black coffee." She laughs that rough laugh again, and Anna joins in politely.

Her first question, after we settle in, is what the show is about. We've had to discuss this before when Ray was helping us put together the posters, so Anna takes this one, smoothly laying out some scant details about Elise and Julian, about memory and the turns that life takes.

Cassandra takes a swig of her coffee, and I stare at the series of red crescents her lipstick is leaving on the mug. "So what's your biggest fear, performing a show like this?"

"Biggest fear?" Anna asks.

"Sure, I mean, have you thought about how hard it might be to perform such personal material?" I can see Anna is a little panicked, searching for an answer, so I step in.

"Um, I think this kind of stuff, you know, is always personal." God, I sound like such a moron. "What I mean is, sure, it might feel a little, um, raw sometimes. But I think it's also been cathartic, finding a way to talk about things that are normally hard to bring up in conversation."

"In rehearsal, you mean," Cassandra says. "Might it be different in front of a crowd?"

"Anna and I are both performers," I say firmly. "Even though this material can be emotionally loaded, we wrote it to be performed, because that's who we are." There, that was a little better. Anna glances at me gratefully over the rim of her cup while Cassandra scribbles something in her notebook.

"You mention performing," she says, setting down her pen. "Tell me a little about your previous artistic endeavors and how they compare to this one. Anna, you were a classical violinist, right?"

"That's right," Anna says. "I loved playing in my school orchestra, I loved that feeling of collaboration, but I felt like I was reaching the limit of what I was capable of there. It wasn't fun anymore, and that kind of practice was starting to wear on my body, on the tendons in my wrist. Rehearsing now feels very natural and more creative, and I think it's because the material has so much of me in it." I'm about to add to this, but Anna keeps talking. "And you know, it's funny, because I don't think anyone would have considered Liam and me to be very much alike, but I think we came together because we were, artistically, in such similar situations. He was in a band, but it had totally stalled out creatively. And when I went to their show, it was impossible to hear Liam in the music." She turns to me. "Right?"

I feel sucker punched. I think of her coming to that show;

I think of the connection between us, the butterflies in my stomach and my hesitance to look directly at her, like I would be staring into the brilliance of the sun. "I mean, I wrote those songs, too," I mutter. "But yeah, the band is on a little bit of a hiatus right now."

"What's the name of your band, Liam?" Cassandra asks brightly, as though the friction between us has invigorated her. The terrible thing is that the band has had so many names and I'm so distracted by Anna's traitorous assessment of my music that the correct answer vanishes in a blip from my mind.

"It's, um, it's…"

"The band was called the Straitjackets," Anna supplies helpfully.

"The band is called the Straitjackets," I say.

Cassandra has a few more questions for us, though I have a hard time focusing, and then she downs the rest of her drink and abruptly stands up. "Break a leg out there, kids!" she says. "I can't wait to see the show."

While walking to the parking lot, my blood is pounding so hard that I feel like one giant heartbeat, consumed by the pulse of something hot and fleshy. "Why would you say that about my band?" I finally manage to spit out. I reach out and pull on her hand, and it spins her around to face me, confusion written all over her. "I remember you coming to that show. I remember how much you said you liked it."

"What?" She is bewildered. She didn't say it out of malice, then, but I'm not sure that makes me feel much better. "Liam, I did like that show. I didn't say anything in the interview that indicated I didn't. I guess I just…I wanted to express how different this feels than any of the stuff we've done before. That's all."

Her tone is so calm and measured that it spins me in the opposite direction. "You don't get to tell a reporter or anyone else how I feel about anything," I yell.

So I've come to this; I am yelling at her in a parking lot. A middle-aged woman walking into the coffee shop gives me a long, hard look. I drop Anna's hand and take a step back. I look down at my boots and fold my arms, and the woman continues on her way, but my teeth are still gritted. "The band still exists. It didn't just disappear because you and I started working together."

"Liam," Anna says, and waits for me to look at her, but I refuse to give her the satisfaction. "Liam, I'm sorry I said that. It was dumb."

"I never would have talked shit on your classical music. Never."

"Well," Anna says. "Actually. You've never heard me play classical. You never asked."

We are both silent for a beat. She's right, of course, but the fury inside me still hasn't subsided.

"Look," she says, "if anything, all the work and the heart you've poured into this show will make the music you write for the band even stronger. That's the truth. And I'm not trying to make you into one thing. I just want the world to know that what we made together is really special."

Her words are like a pail of water thrown on the flames within me, but they leave behind a sodden ash heap of sadness. I want to hide somewhere for a day or two, not perform my life story in front of a crowd. I turn my back and ignore her as she calls my name with increasing degrees of desperation. My father's stupid SUV has such a well-made and quiet engine that I can still hear her calling to me, even as I turn the key and drive away.

For a long time, I drive without a destination. I don't want to go home or to any of my usual writing spots, because I don't want Anna to track me down and force me to talk it out. I'm not hungry, and the thought of sitting in any sort of coffee shop makes me feel antsy. I even consider, briefly, going to the cemetery where Julian is buried so I can talk at the gravestone like they do in weepy, softheaded films, but the truth is, my parents have never been the visiting-the-gravesite sort of mourners, and I'm not even positive I can find Julian's headstone, a failure that would be as depressing as the impulse to find it in the first place is embarrassing. Instead, I drive and drive, avoiding the interstate, sticking to winding country routes that I've never seen before. To do a show like this with someone who understands me so little is impossible. I'll walk away from all of it. I'll call Ray and cancel the whole thing.

I drive for hours, until I'm almost out of gas, but when I find a place to fill up and ask directions, I realize that I must have been driving in circles, because I'm only about forty minutes outside of Mercer. On the way back, I find myself passing Gavin's house. On an impulse, I stop, not really expecting him to be there, but he is, and we sit on the front porch for a few minutes, talking about music, about the band.

"You guys been practicing without me?" I ask, trying to keep the panic out of my voice. Eric told me at the last minute that they had planned a practice for Friday night, but I had, of course, been rehearsing with Anna.

"Nah, not really," Gavin says. "Eric never showed, so that left me and Chris, who was really into giving me advice on how to play drums." He rolls his eyes in such a soft Gavin way that it's more of an eyebrow raise. "Let's just say you were missed."

"Sorry," I say. "Maybe we can get something together this week."

"Yeah, for sure. Kinda surprised to hear you say that, though, with the show going up this week. You guys have a fight or something?"

God, this town. You can't take a shit without someone gossiping about it. "Where'd you hear that?" I ask.

"Just a guess," Gavin says. "But is it true?"

"There is no show," I tell him. "I don't know why I always step right into the things that are bad for me."

"Come on, man," Gavin says. "Everyone's been talking about that coffee shop performance ever since it happened. Like...everyone. Saying it was like watching a star being born or something. When you first pulled up to the house, I thought you came here to tell me you were out of the band for good."

I can't help but feel a momentary wave of pleasure at the thought that people were paying attention, but then the silt of the day's shitstorm settles back down on me.

"I don't know," I say. "I miss the band. I feel like I'm not being true to myself, doing this stuff with Anna."

"Oh, I see," Gavin says, laughing a little, and this time rolling his eyes for real. "You came here so I could tell you not to be such an asshole."

"No, you don't get it," I start to say, but Gavin waves me off.

"Well, just in case you do need it, here you go: I love you, Liam, but you really are an asshole." Gavin stands up and holds out his hand for us to knock fists, and then he makes it clear that he's not going to continue this conversation. "And if you blow this opportunity for the chance to listen to Chris explain why Jimmy Page is a hack for the eightieth time this year, then— I'm serious, Liam—I will probably never forgive you." Gavin stretches, then shoots an imaginary gun at me while making a pinging sound and goes into the house without another word.

Shit. Gavin's version of tough love, I guess.

I drive home, knowing that there's truth to what he said,

but there's truth to what I've been feeling all day, too. I love Anna, and I hate her, too. That two seemingly contradictory things can be equally true—I'm not sure why no one else seems torn apart by it like I am.

When my mother tells me in the morning, somewhat pointedly, that Anna left numerous messages for me the night before, I can't bring myself to call her, but I don't call the Greenville Playhouse to tell them the whole thing is canceled, either. I'm almost afraid to pick up the phone, uncertain of which number I would find myself dialing.

All day I feel suspended between extremes, unable to know which is the right one, and then I go home again and find a package on the front porch. Inside is a black T-shirt, hand-silk-screened with bright yellow-green paint to read THE STRAITJACKETS in heavy-metal font. There's also a note that says, "I'll be your band groupie whenever you want me to be. Forgive me."

I consider the restraint it took for Anna not to mention the show in this note, even though it's the thing she cares most about in the whole world. For a moment, a feeling that lies ever dormant within me becomes a clear thought in my head: I wish that Julian were the one left behind, the one responsible for navigating this complicated world, the one who has to fix everything that I have broken.

I'm worried, on the drive to Anna's house, about what I will say when she opens the door, but when it actually happens, we are kissing each other before either of us can speak. I know that we are kissing to erase the need for words, but for once, I am relieved by silence. Usually we practice in the cluttered living room, pushing stacks of library books and newspapers out of the way, the whole space smelling vaguely of old dog. But today Anna leads me down the hall to her room.

"I thought you had disappeared forever," Anna says, helping me untangle my arms from my shirt and then pulling her own sweater over her head.

"I thought you had forgotten who I was," I say. I take a moment to drink in the sight of her, try to imprint it on my brain to use the next time I feel crazy: those familiar lips, the graceful curve of her collarbone, the fullness of her breasts under her blue bra. Then we are pressed together again, my lips on her neck, her shoulder, her arms circling my ribs and pulling me over onto the yellow-and-blue quilt of her bed.

"Never," she says, lying on her side with her face so close to mine that I can see each of her eyelashes separately. "I know you better than anyone." Then she rolls on top of me, the pressure of her body erasing the thoughts of the past two days.

How nice it would be, how easy, if we could both simply memorize the contents of the other's soul the same way we memorize song lyrics. I cling to her and let all the words wash away from us.

17

TO THE LEFT

THE NEXT DAY ELISE is missing from school, and I have to assume that she is once again off with Eric, appreciating nature while also imbibing some sort of illegal substance. (Where were they this time? Snorting cocaine on the peak of a mountain? Doing ecstasy while skin diving for pearls?) This time I have too much on my mind to be quite as worried as before. Also, ever since we were small children, Elise has been able to sniff out any tiny morsel of knowledge that I have tried to hide from her, so I actually experience a flutter of relief that I won't have to tell her quite yet that I saw Liam last night, that we argued about her, or that I woke this morning thinking not of Sergei or even of gross Mr. Foster, but of Liam's face, the way he tilts his head down and looks up at me through his thick black eyelashes when he asks me a question and how the eye contact makes me feel as if I am the only person on the planet.

The day drags on and on with a deadening heaviness. My arm aches endlessly after last night's rehearsal, and I'm dying to get home so I can ice it. Mr. Carson gives me a sidelong glance when he sees that Elise is missing again, but this time he doesn't ask me anything about it. After I do finally get home and ice my arm and then practice for a couple hours (I *will* be better than Sergei, I will), I realize that I've been half expecting Elise to burst into my bedroom exactly as she did the week before, and when she doesn't, an unease creeps again to the front of my mind. I wander out into the kitchen, where my parents are in the middle of making dinner together.

"Fajitas!" my dad announces happily, then kisses me on the forehead. "And maybe even mint chocolate chip ice cream for dessert if we manage to clean our plates." Sometimes I'm not sure if my father remembers that I am almost an adult, because nothing about our relationship seems to have changed since I was approximately seven years old. He looks so cheerful, though, that I attempt to smile at him while he goes back to grating cheese.

"How was rehearsal last night, my love?" my mother asks.

I momentarily consider telling her the truth or at least some small portion of it, but then I get bogged down in the question of what rotten part to reveal: the constant pressure to measure up, the aggression I feel toward Sergei, the complicating presence of Liam, the fact that I no longer have a private violin teacher and why, or even the pain in my arm. Trying to untangle these threads makes me feel like I'm stuck in a spider's web, though, so instead I say: "It was fine."

The phone rings then, and I feel certain that it is Elise, especially when my mother answers it and says, "Sure, sure, she's right here." But then she mouths, "Elise's mom," and my heart stalls. Elise's mother has never, ever called me on the phone, and there's no conceivable explanation aside from something awful that I cannot bring myself to name.

"Um, hello?" I breathe into the receiver.

"Anna, it's Caroline," she says, and I brace myself for some terrible piece of news that I could have potentially averted, but her next words are: "Don't worry, you're not in trouble." This is exactly the sort of thing that adults say when you are in a lot of trouble, but even so, it eases me a little, since it's not an announcement of disaster. "Do you know where Elise might have gone today?"

"I..." My mind swirls. It's still pretty early in the evening, so why is Elise's mom obviously trying not to sound freaked out? They've learned something that made them worry, that is clear. Has the school caught on to the absence scheme? Or maybe Mr. Carson called Elise's parents directly? That wasn't exactly within school protocol, but Mr. Carson was old-school, too close to retirement to care about following the rules if he thought they were dumb. "Isn't she home yet?" I ask, stalling.

"No," she says. "No one has seen her since this morning. We know you weren't with her, but did she mention anything to you? Anywhere she might have been thinking about going?"

I can tell that Elise's mom is working hard to keep her voice calm and even, and I genuinely want to help her, but the truth is that Elise didn't tell me anything about where she was going today. God, where was she? "I'm not sure. I mean, she didn't say anything. Or...she mentioned hiking a while ago, but I'm not sure where."

"Hiking?" Her mother sounds merely curious, not disbelieving, probably used to Elise having strange hobbies she's never heard about. "Okay, well, that's something. We can check the parking lots at local trailheads." I can hear her cover the receiver with her hand, say something to someone, surely Elise's dad, and then she comes back on the line and sighs. "All right, Rick is going to drive around and check those parking lots. That's helpful, Anna." I squirm; I know what's coming next, the inevitable squeeze for info, and I know what I'm going to have to do.

Elise's mom is saying: "Anna, is there anyone else who might know where she is? We know you care about Elise as much as we do, and we just want to make sure that we have all the information." There is a heavy pause. Elise is going to be so mad at me. She is never going to forgive me. "Please, Anna."

I blurt it out, get it over with: "You should talk to Eric. I mean, I don't know for sure that she was with him today, but I know that they went hiking together...before. So maybe she said something to him that she didn't say to me. A...a location or something."

"Eric. Okay. Okay. And how can we reach Eric? Do you have his phone number? His last name, maybe?"

"No," I say, and consider leaving it there, but I know that won't stop the flood of questions—how we met Eric, where he goes to school—and I just want this to end, want to know that Elise is safe. I close my eyes. "You could ask Liam. I think they're friends. I mean...they're friends. He's the one who came with us to that concert once."

"Oh yes, right," she says. "Liam. Huh."

And then, miraculously, as if conjured by my decision to snitch, there's some noise on the other end of the line, a conversation with multiple voices involved, and I am positive that I hear Elise's voice among them.

Elise's mom is back on the phone, her voice completely altered by the release of tension: "She's here. She walked in as her dad was about to go out." There's some more talking in the background. "I have to go. Thank you for your help, Anna. Everything's going to be okay." And then she hangs up.

My eyes are still closed. I'm imagining the scene at Elise's house right now, wondering if she is in a similar state as when she passed out in my bedroom last week, wondering

190

how much of the phone call Caroline will relay to Elise. It doesn't matter. Elise will know exactly who mentioned Eric's name.

When I open my eyes and slowly set down the receiver, I realize that my parents have stopped cooking and are both staring at me. Twyla wanders into the kitchen, almost knocking over her water dish because she's so blind, then begins to slurp from it noisily.

"Is everything all right, Anna?" my mom asks.

"Yeah," I say weakly. "Elise was late getting home, but she's there now." The idea of unburdening myself to them, of figuring out a way of putting down the load of trash that my life has been this past week—it is too much a burden in itself. Instead, I will eat the fajitas, I will listen to my parents chat happily to each other, I will swallow the tortillas and peppers as though they are feelings, and then I will drag my invisible but growing pile of garbage off to bed.

No matter how much I tell myself that I don't care if Elise is furious with me, that I did what any reasonable person would do, that I am prepared to weather the storm of Elise's emotions until they pass, it still hurts when I spot Elise at her locker and am met with a stony silence when I tell her how glad I am that she's back. Elise slams her locker with a crash and puts her face close to mine. I can see how the purple shadows under Elise's eyes have darkened, and the lids are puffy as though she's been crying.

"I don't have anything to say to traitors," Elise says loudly enough for others to overhear.

My throat closes, and Elise whirls on her heel. I can hear murmurs and one low whistle from the people standing nearby.

It's not fair, I want to tell everyone. It's not fair that when I'm angry or irritated with Elise, I smother it, and when I'm on the receiving end, I bear it like a stoic while she publicly insults me. But I also believe, deep down, that there is something terribly wrong with me that I have ended up in this situation, that some essential flaw of character has led me not only to this uneven friendship, but to this exact place in the world. I am not a traitor, I know this deep in my gut, but I might be so loyal that it will destroy me.

In the days leading up to the orchestra's winter concert, I do not speak to Elise. All the time I might have spent hanging out with her I instead pour into practicing. I wage war against the music, and my left arm screams out like a casualty of battle, but I'm doing it; I'm winning. I imagine hacking my forearm off with a samurai sword, sliding it through the hole in a guillotine, waving a white flag with it until someone blasts it off anyway with a round of mortar fire. I have always assumed that I will grit my teeth and come out on the other side of this pain somehow, but perhaps that is impossible.

Perhaps the agony will be with me always. Perhaps Elise will never forgive me.

The week before the concert, I have another date with Sergei, this one on a Friday, without rehearsal to hurry to afterward. He takes me to a restaurant, a nice one, and I order pasta, but everything tastes like sawdust in my mouth. I refuse to speak of the violin or the orchestra at all on this date, resolve to make a point that there is more to me than that. I will definitely not mention Elise or Call-Me-Gary or Liam; I have no interest in hearing him give me advice on how to feel or what to prioritize. Sergei looks baffled by the stilted conversation.

After dinner, I walk wordlessly out of the restaurant and climb uninvited into the back seat of his car, and we make out right there in the parking lot. The concern in Sergei's face drops away, just as I suspected it would. When he slips his hand under my shirt and unfastens my bra, all I feel is the fire in my left arm. The rest of me is deadened, wooden, as though I am only acting out what has, all along, been preordained. All these years, I thought I'd been trying to make good on my miraculous landing, but the truth is, I've never stopped falling.

18

TO THE RIGHT

ON THE DAY THE show is to open, I fumble my way through every class, ignoring whole lectures and surely bombing a trigonometry quiz. It doesn't matter. All that matters is that at least a dozen people stop me and tell me they have tickets for the show.

Anna and I met yesterday and repeatedly ran through the show, each time nearly flawless. But I insisted that we not rehearse today, that we come to the material fresh. It's a habit I developed for rock shows to give the music that vital kick of energy. I could tell that the suggestion made Anna worry that we'll make some error that rehearsal could have prevented or maybe even that I will lose my mind and not show up to the theater. "Trust me," I told her, and though I could see from the struggle that flickered across her face that she didn't, I also knew that she was trying to, and for now, that would have to be enough.

I drive to my father's office, a place I actively avoid most of the time, and make the extra effort of picking up two lemonades from a café that he likes. Now or never. But Rebecca, his secretary, says he's in a meeting that will last until the end of the day, and then she tells me to break a leg. I leave one of the lemonades for Rebecca and sip the other one in the parked car, feeling the pull of Anna nervously waiting for me somewhere out there, the invisible connection that tethers us to each other across space.

I was surprised when Anna first suggested a couple weeks ago that we should mingle in the lobby with the audience members rather than wait backstage. That's exactly the sort of improvised banter that she hates. But she had been adamant that the show needed to feel like a conversation with friends, that we needed to appear as natural as possible, rather than like performers held at a distance. Now I can see that she was completely right, that people love the fact that the two of us are milling around out here, drinking bottles of water from the concession stand and chatting with everyone like regular audience members. Anna is talking to a couple cellists from her school orchestra, and I'm talking with Gavin and Eric about Eric's terrible idea for a song that comes with instructions to get high before you're allowed to listen to it when Muriel walks in. She's by herself, wearing a long green jacket, and she looks very put together. She looks great, if I'm being honest. I steel my nerves and walk over to say hello.

"Liam," she says. "I can't believe it. This is so exciting." She gives my arm a squeeze, and the contact makes my heart beat harder, like the muscle itself is remembering her.

"It's very cool of you to come," I say. "You didn't have to."

"Of course I didn't *have* to," she says, and there it is, that nervous but musical laugh. "I wanted to." Over her shoulder, I see my parents walk in. My father's face darkens at the sight of Muriel, whom he never liked. My mom guides him directly toward the concession stand, where she's probably going to buy them some wine, and I feel a momentary twinge of guilt and anxiety that I didn't try harder and earlier to have a real conversation with my father about the show.

"You look happy," I say to Muriel, which isn't exactly true, but she doesn't look nearly as miserable as when she was with me. She laughs again.

"I guess you could say that. I've started running cross-country. Can you believe that? Me, an athlete? My shrink suggested it. She's really good."

"That's...great," I say. I always loved that about her, how bald she was about her emotions. I wonder briefly if we could have made it work—if she'd been a little less tortured, if I'd been a little more patient.

I'm saved from this reverie by an announcement asking that people please take their seats. Muriel squeezes my arm again and tells me to break a leg, and then she's gone, walking toward the theater entrance.

I locate Anna and make my way toward her. She is wearing the blue dress she'd worn when I first saw her at the funeral home; her hair is pulled back from her face in a way that is simple but pretty, and she's wearing more makeup than usual. For a second, there is a panic of nonrecognition, that same disconnected falling feeling that I had while I listened to her say those things about the band. For a second, I am a ghost particle. But then she's next to me, smelling familiar, the feel of her hand on the back of my neck as she leans to my ear to say, "It's our secret for a few seconds longer—how much everyone is going to love this show."

Most of the time she says perfect things. I know this. I wish we could run away from here and make out, not only because I desire the curve of her hips and the hollow of her neck, though that is part of it, but also to remind myself that we are real, that the connection between us is real and not something I create with my mind when I feel lost in the world. Instead, I rest my cheek against hers, imagining our brain waves becoming synced, the amplitudes lining up and adding together, and then we hold hands and drift into the theater with the last of the crowd.

We walk nonchalantly to the stage, and I climb up first

and then help her follow. The staging is supremely simple: Two chairs, Anna's violin case, the pedals to control the playback, a couple monitors, the circulatory system of cables. A dark gray backdrop that is lit subtly with different colors during different parts of the show. Microphones.

We sit, the audience quiets, and we wait for the first sound cue. It's a low click and then a staticky whirring that gets louder, the sound of an audiocassette turning, and then Elise's voice doing her radio announcer act: "Well, hey there, listeners. We've got an outstanding show for you tonight, jam-packed with all the music you've been waiting to hear. So keep your radio and your dancing shoes on, and don't even think about turning that dial." The sound of her voice slowly fades, and Anna starts to play the main theme that we've written, the phrase that will be woven throughout the show in a dozen different ways. It's so pretty, the notes showing off her vibrato, the round sound of it echoing through the theater in a way that warms my blood.

I lean into the microphone in front of my chair and say: "What do you do when you hear the voice of a ghost? When the voice is the most familiar sound in the world?"

Anna puts the melody on a loop and starts talking. "The first time I saw Elise, I was at a swimming class at the YMCA. We were five. She had a pink two-piece swimsuit, and she always, always won the contests to see who could hold their breath the longest. I mean, who wouldn't want to be her friend?" The audience laughs a little. We're off to a smooth start. Anna's voice sounds great, the right combination of fragile and smooth. I listen to her finish this opening monologue about Elise, and then she begins to play again, and she's so good that it feels like the audience is breathing along with the music. It's so easy to open my mouth and sing: "Ghosts who float in on the evening air, ghosts who get tangled up in your hair, ghosts who knock around inside your head, ghosts who come lie beside you in bed."

It isn't until right before my own monologue that I feel a momentary clench of stage fright, feel it suck at the air inside my lungs. It almost feels like a dream when Anna leans into the microphone to say: "What do you do when you hear the voice of a ghost? When the voice isn't as familiar as it should be?" and then it's a snippet of Julian's voice playing over the sound system, his wind-chime-like, childish voice repeating some Seussian rhyme: "Barber, baby, bubbles, and a bumble-bee!" and then squealing with laughter.

I feel a surge of vertigo and want to close my eyes. Instead, I turn to a trick a drama teacher taught me once, training my eyes to the dark back of the auditorium, giving the illusion of making eye contact without running the risk of having to see any one person in the audience, especially my father.

"I don't remember my brother sounding this young. That's because I wasn't born yet. No one even imagined my existence, especially not my parents, until Julian was older. According to all my sources, though, everyone loved Julian. He was one of those quirky little kids who became momentarily obsessed with all kinds of things, and he would share facts, lots of facts, with total strangers: dinosaurs, LEGOs, dogs, airplanes. I would know so much more about aerodynamics right now if I'd been around back then for Julian to teach me. Later, he got sick, really sick, and he knew all the facts about that, too: lymphocytes, blast cells, relapse. It's hard to keep a smart kid from knowing stuff like that." I can't tell if I'm doing a good job or a terrible one; I only know that the words are out there now, reverberating in the ears of the audience. Stupid Cassandra St. Claire—she was right. It's harder to say this in front of a lot of people. Keep going, just get to the end. "Everyone loved Julian so much that they tried to find a bone marrow match, and when that didn't work, they tried to make one. And what they made was me."

I turn to look at Anna then, and she's looking at me with something pure, though I'm not sure if it's love or respect or pity. I know, though, that the eye contact between us is what will keep me afloat. As much as possible, for the rest of the show, we look at each other, even when Anna is playing, even when I am singing. This is the way we swim through the rest of the show, that invisible rope between us now so short that we can both almost see and touch it.

We talk and sing and play all the parts we have written

together: all the memories about Elise and Julian, and the material about what music means to us, and the hard punch, the full stop, when we tell the audience with the simplest, shortest sentences about what happened to Elise and Julian. And then, the music starts again, slowly and quietly, a tiny snippet of Beethoven's "Für Elise" that morphs into our own song, and then we talk about what it was like to write the show together, about how it feels to be the ones who are still here, and finally, one last return to the audiotape, an outtake from the radio show we wrote with Elise as kids.

There's the sound of Anna saying, "How about this?" and then playing some crappy keyboard, her nine-year-old fingers pounding out a melody that mimics classic rock and roll. "That's so good!" Elise yells, and then there's my voice crooning a spoof of Del Shannon's "Runaway," "I'm a walkin' with some pain; Got run over by a train," and then the peal of the little girls' laughter fading out and away.

"See, the ghosts you don't think of as much are the ghosts of yourself," I say. "The ghost of who you were and all the ghosts of who you could have become, if just one thing was different. Or if everything was different. Some days, it's hard to know which version of yourself is the real one. That's why you have to find the people who can help you remember." Anna plays the melody from the top of the show, ending on one final note that slides into silence with a shiver.

We've done it, we've made it to the finish line. The show

is compact, not much more than an hour, but it feels like enough. It feels like a lifetime.

Anna reaches out her hand and we stand up together to take a bow. The house lights are coming up, and as they do, I see my father wipe his eyes. He is the first one out of his seat, not to flee the theater, but to applaud us. Then everyone is standing, clapping, smiling. A sea of appreciation wherever I look.

I turn to look at Anna again, beautiful under the lights. I chose her above all else, and this is the result. This is what it feels like to be on top of the world.

19

TO THE LEFT

THE VENUE FOR THE concert is a big, beautiful theater, the same place where my mother used to take me to *The Nutcracker* each Christmas season as a special treat.

"You're in lights!" my father announces exuberantly as they drop me off that afternoon, and it's true—there are the details of the concert displayed on the theater's marquee. I feel only dread, though, as I open the door and go inside for our final brief dress rehearsal. I have a boyfriend I barely care about, a best friend who definitely will not show up to the most important concert of my life, and an all-consuming pursuit that regularly brings me physical agony. It doesn't help that everywhere I look, everyone is wearing black suits, black dresses; it's the traditional formal concert attire, but right now it looks more like funeral wear. There are signs directing us to rehearsal rooms in the basement, where we can leave our coats and instrument cases, and if anyone had told me six months ago that this is where I would be, allowed entrance to the inner sanctum of this theater as a performer, I would have assumed that my emotion would be utter jubilation, the glee of a victor. Instead, I feel numb, like someone has affixed a mute to the strings vibrating inside me.

Sergei is warming up downstairs, and I have a few moments to spy on him. He's wearing a suit that looks like it was stolen from the set of a Beatles movie, the pants tighter and the tie skinnier than anyone else in the room. He has gotten a haircut, the shorter hairs sticking up in a bristly, untamed way. I can't decide if his style is charmingly unexpected or simply strange. Thinking about the fact that the same hands that are playing those scales were feeling me up in the back of a car last week makes me feel even more flattened, dampened. I dump everything except my violin and bow in a heap and hurry to the staircase leading to the backstage area before he can spot me.

It's very dark and cool in the theater, and some combination of nerves and temperature sets me to shivering uncontrollably. I should have borrowed one of my mother's black sweaters. I walk out onto the stage, which is set up but empty of people, and sit down in my chair, and for a few minutes, I feel like I can breathe again. It's like surfacing from deep, cold water, and for a split second, my mind flashes back to my first glimpse of Elise, emerging from the YMCA pool, gasping for breath, but also sleek and magnificent, almost glowing. I can't help it; I want her here so badly.

Someone has placed a copy of the evening's program on each stand, and I page through it. When I see the full program, the combination seems extremely dark: The Saint-Saëns about the doomed Samson, the Strauss tone poem about death, Liam's aria in the voice of a murderous clown. I'm not even sure what the Bartók is supposed to be about, but everything he wrote sort of sounds like an axe murderer showed up to a family barbecue. It suddenly seems deeply ominous that I've been playing these pieces for weeks and never recognized the bleak picture they were painting.

Sergei sneaks up behind me (I hear him coming but decide to ignore it) and slips his hands over my eyes. "Basking in the imagined applause?" he whispers near my head, and then bites my earlobe clumsily. I try not to wince. He takes his hands away and sits in Michelle's seat. "I'm surprised you didn't sit down in my seat, since you're working so hard to take it." He says this cheerfully enough, but the truth in it rankles.

"What's that supposed to mean?" I snap, but by now there are lots of people wandering out to the stage to take their seats for rehearsal.

"Move it, Master Igor," Michelle says, walking over to us and giving Sergei's shoe a kick. "I want to sit down." He stays seated for a beat and grins at her.

"You're such a bitch, Michelle," he says, and then stands up and gestures grandly at her chair, before turning to me. "You look beautiful today, by the way," he says before walking into the wings. And here is one more reason to be jealous of him, the way he can simply brush off Michelle without letting her under his skin. Why is it that I always have to care more about everything than anyone else in the room?

Mr. Halloway, dressed sharply in a tuxedo, takes to the stage to get the rehearsal going and gestures for Sergei to come tune the orchestra. We practice a few difficult spots first, and the whole orchestra sounds like a skittish horse racing along, well-trained but not quite in control. The cold does nothing to help my arm. I try to stretch it between songs, but it feels like there are thick, frozen rubber bands in there. It doesn't matter. Getting through things is what I do best.

When Liam, also dressed in a tuxedo, comes onto the stage, I have to swallow an audible response. He looks so good, like the suave lead of an old black-and-white movie, and when we rehearse his solo for the last time, his voice is so relaxed and confident, the exact opposite of the way my day is going. As he exits the stage, walking right past Michelle, his eyes fall on me. I'm not imagining that he's glaring at me. What gives? I'm too muted to wonder for longer than a few seconds.

It's during the run-through of the final piece, the last movement of the New World Symphony, that it happens.

During the crashing finale, when I am playing high on the E string, I feel something rip, like something in my arm has come unzipped. It is an atomic bomb followed by a consuming burn. I let out a small cry, but it's mostly drowned out by the cacophony.

"And now, applause, applause, applause," Mr. Halloway is saying from some distant place as he has the orchestra practice taking a bow, but all I can see is an erupting volcano of pain.

"What's up with you?" Michelle asks from somewhere far above, and it's only then that I realize I'm not on my feet like everyone else. My legs feel shaky. I hold both my bow and violin with my right hand, not sure how to move my left arm to slow the lava. The pain is worse than all the elaborate deaths I have imagined for this arm. The reality of it is terrible, insistent, suffocating.

"Okay, folks," I hear Mr. Halloway say. "You've worked hard this semester, so let's really show them what we've got tonight. You're going to be great." He says some other things, about there being snacks and drinks set up downstairs for us until showtime, about how we need to keep the noise level down as they open the theater doors. I can't process any of it. The pain has put me in a full-body sweat. As soon as we're dismissed, I leap from my seat, hoping that I can sit in a quiet bathroom stall and figure out what to do. As I'm walking through the wings, however, someone grabs me hard by the elbow, almost knocking the instrument out of my hand, and it spins me around. At least it's my right arm that Liam is clutching, not the one that is a conflagration of agony.

"It was you, wasn't it?" he says, tugging me into a dark corner behind one of the side curtains. "Eric mopes around all day, refusing to come to band practice because he says the world has no meaning without Elise." Over Liam's shoulder, I can see the rest of the orchestra members walking past on their way downstairs to eat pretzels and drink soda. There are also some adults, mostly teachers or musicians who help manage the orchestra, and, chatting to Mr. Halloway's wife, is Call-Me-Gary, looking perfectly relaxed and telling her something that's causing her to chuckle.

"You couldn't stay out of it, could you?" Liam is saying. "You don't even trust your best friend enough to let her make her own mistakes."

"Wasn't me," I mumble, though I don't have the energy to make my tongue move properly. "Some teacher told her parents, probably. I mentioned Eric, but they would have figured it out anyway."

"There's a ripple effect to any action," he gripes, "one ripple being that my band is barely a band at this point."

I'm in the middle of a major crisis, and I'm still listening to everyone else's problems. "Don't you have better things to do than yell at me? Sing a solo in front of hundreds of people, find a reliable bass player, et cetera?"

While I'm saying this, Sergei walks past looking like he doesn't have a care in the world. I see in a flash that I will never be the violinist he is. I care too much. This thought, combined with the pain, is too much to handle standing up, and I take a step backward, sensing a wall there that I can lean on. It's only a curtain, though, and I lose my balance, one knee buckling, and then I'm falling.

"Are you...," Liam says, reaching out to steady me, and then says something like, "Oh. Oh. Whoa there," when he sees that I can't really hold myself upright anymore.

It's over. It's really, truly over this time. I am the one who makes it through, and I can't make it through this. The idea of sitting down and playing an entire concert right now is inconceivable. I let my violin fall from my arm, just drop it on the ground, where it makes a crashing sound that is strangely musical.

"Are you okay?" Liam asks, but the idea that I am okay is so laughable that I do not bother to answer but instead laugh, which sounds high-pitched and out of control, even to me.

"Liam," I say, holding on to him with my bad arm, the tightened grip narrowing and intensifying the fire in a molten core. My cheeks feel wet, even though for once I don't remember having the impulse to cry. "Why is life such fucking garbage all the time?" He smiles at that, even though his brow is furrowed—of course it is, there being a collapsed near-stranger in his arms.

In that moment, right before he has time to call for help, that's when I kiss him. The decision doesn't make any sense, and I can only explain it to myself as an acute need to grab hold of something, a last-ditch effort to pull myself up out of the despair.

He doesn't pull away, which is fortunate, since I would fall on the floor alongside my violin without him. Instead, all the noise and static and movement and even most of the pain drop away from us for a moment, and we stand there with our lips pressed together, joined together in the stillness, outside the laws of time. I can feel all the spots of contact between us—our mouths, our arms, our chests—come alive, electrified, as though our bodies are exchanging particles. It's not that I'm falling; I am a vibrating wave. I am everywhere and nowhere.

Later, I will have to find the strength to stand on my own again, I will have to offer Liam a flustered apology, I will have to pick up my violin and get the hell out of this theater, I will have to find someone to amputate my left arm and put me out of my misery, I will have to flee the country in order to avoid seeing Liam again and to avoid reliving this intense moment for the rest of my life.

But not yet, not yet.

Life is hard / And so am I.

—MARK OLIVER EVERETT, front man of
the rock band Eels and son of quantum
physicist Hugh Everett

20

TO THE RIGHT

THE WEEKLONG RUN OF the show is so full of its own momentum and energy that I can feel every cell, every atom, in my body spinning toward some dizzying conclusion. Every night my mind buzzes until it is almost dawn. Ray allows us to add an extra show, then two, until we absolutely cannot extend it any further and must vacate the stage for a production of *Arsenic and Old Lace* starring, among others, my former kindergarten teacher. I am sad to see it end but also exhausted and relieved.

That first night after our run has ended, I suggest to Anna that we go to the park where we had some of our first timid rehearsals of the show. It seems like a good way to bring things full circle and a good way to be alone with her, but Anna makes a face, says it's gotten so cold, and couldn't we meet at Higher Grounds instead?

So here I am, eating chocolate-covered espresso beans to stay awake until my skin feels like it is vibrating in an unpleasant way. Anna is pressing her knee against mine under the table, which is nice, but I still feel a little surly that this is the place she chose. The last time we were here, of course, was the occasion of the betrayal. When the interview was published, the focus was on the two of us, how we composed the show after not seeing each other since childhood. The band was barely mentioned. Even so, I still find myself getting caught up in a subordinate clause in which it was referred to as my "failed rock band," a wince-worthy phrase and one I hope that Chris won't see before we resume band practices.

But all of this is just self-indulgent whining, I guess. It's not a quality of mine that I like, this tendency to fixate on the negative and mope about it, so I try, really try, to lift myself out of it. There are plenty of positive things to think of, after all. Onstage, we had been unstoppable. Aunt Caroline came to one of the performances and bawled her way through it, but afterward she clung to both Anna and me, saying, "For an hour, you gave her back to me." And though my father hasn't really discussed the content of the show with me, he seems to have curbed his usual nitpicking—during one of the final performances, I saw that he had slipped into the back row, watching it all by himself.

And now, here is Anna, looking happier than I've ever seen her, telling me that she has a surprise for me.

"A surprise?" I ask. "Good surprise or bad surprise?"

"Good," Anna says, reaching out to squeeze one of my hands. "Very good." Despite her words, my heart thumps heavily. Probably just the espresso beans, I tell myself. "The manager of the Circle Tour Theater in Columbus called me this morning. They want to book *Ghost Melodies* for a week-long stint in December. It's not too much bigger than the playhouse, but I looked it up and it's such a cool space—a thrust stage, beautiful acoustics."

"December," I say. "That's only a couple weeks away."

"Yeah, but he said they loved the show and wouldn't require many changes to what we're already doing. Liam," she says, narrowing her eyes at me, "this is good news. Really good news."

"You're right," I say, even though there's a stone sinking down, down, down, through the center of me. I feel the grip of her hand relax a little. "I think I'm worn out from being onstage, that's all. And I was looking forward to getting back to band practice, but that can wait. A few days of rest and I won't be able to contain my excitement probably."

Anna suddenly seems extremely preoccupied examining a hangnail on her right thumb. "Yeah. Sure, I'm tired, too. But actually, they really want to see a run-through of the show tomorrow afternoon in the space so they can give us some notes."

"Tomorrow?" I say. "Notes? We have school, though." A

look of disbelief flickers across her face, and I get it. I can barely believe it myself, that I, the self-styled rebel, would treat school as an obstacle to art.

"Yeah, it's just that they can't do it in the evening because there's other stuff going on there. I got permission from my parents already, so I know you'll think of something to tell yours."

I pick up another of the candies and crush it between my molars. I force myself to slow down and swallow before I respond. "You told your parents about this new gig before you told me?"

"Only because I wanted to save it as a surprise for right now," Anna says hurriedly. "I thought it would be appropriate somehow. This was our first venue, after all. The place where we were discovered."

I literally bite my tongue, feeling the muscle flatten and indent along the ridge of my teeth. I know that I'm seeing everything through a filter of gloomy contrariness—I do this sometimes—but really, how can we be soulmates when we differ in so many little ways? The next thought to flicker to life in my brain lowers me even more.

"Why did they call you? Why didn't they ask to meet with both of us?"

Anna sighs, and I can hear exasperation in it. "They found my parents' number in the phone book? I don't know. Look, can we go do this thing tomorrow and talk to them? And I promise if it still seems like a bad idea to you, then we won't do it."

"I didn't say it was a bad idea."

"Yeah, but you're acting like I'm scheming behind your back. I mean, this was a five-minute phone call and three minutes of it was him gushing about how talented we both are." She reaches over to take my hand again, and I churlishly move it beneath the table.

"Liam," she says, "please don't do this."

"Do what?"

The set of her face is unpleasantly hard. "Don't take something beautiful and turn it ugly."

There is a shadow version of me that would throw it back in her face, who would tell her to do the show herself if she can't handle who I am, who would walk out of the café and into the night. But I am better than that. I know that I can rise above, even when people treat me as if I am disposable.

"Well," I say, "let's see how it goes tomorrow, then."

She gets out of her seat and walks to my side of the table and puts her hands on my face. I can feel people at nearby tables looking at us. I know this is not something that Anna would typically do.

"I love you so much," Anna says. "And I want the rest of the world to love you, too."

Even when there's dirt and grit in the space between us, there's life there, too. I can feel it when she kisses me.

On the drive home, I think about how it had been on the tip of my tongue to tell her to go fuck herself. I can't believe I came so close to setting the whole thing on fire, how close I came to flicking a match at a newfound source of happiness that felt like a total revelation only a few weeks before. Sometimes I think I do that kind of shit just to scare myself.

The coffee beans keep my heart racing far into the night. I get up, pace around, try to write lyrics for some band songs, tell myself that I should really get some sleep, and lie twitching in bed for a little while. The cycle repeats until the sky starts to lighten, and then I tumble into a shallow sleep and dream of Muriel.

She is wearing that long green coat and standing in a field of flowers, small flowers in dozens of colors. She keeps trying to pick them, but as soon as she breaks a stem, the bloom in her hand turns gray. She blows on it, trying to revive it, but it only crumbles; frustrated, she throws it down and goes on to the next, which also dies and disintegrates. My dream self knows that if I could only call out to her and tell her the thing that Anna told me—that she shouldn't take something beautiful and make it ugly—her problem would be solved. But instead, she picks faster and faster, wreaking havoc to the whole field. A terrible screeching noise fills the air, and she looks up as though it is a bird or an airplane flying overhead, but then I realize it is only my alarm clock.

I feel like I have not slept at all, which is mostly true. I drag myself to school because my parents insisted that I attend for a half day before leaving for the meeting, and I don't need to add an argument with them to my troubles. By the time I pick up Anna at her school to drive us down to the theater, my eyeballs and skin hurt as though they are too sensitive to be exposed to the world.

The Circle Tour is tucked into the side of a huge shopping complex, a fact that makes me deeply uneasy. The Greenville Playhouse wasn't exactly the center of cutting-edge theater, but at least it's not a stone's throw away from a Cinnabon stall. The manager who called Anna comes out to meet us, and the introduction does little to quell the agitation in my guts. His name is Steve, and he has a mostly gray ponytail and red eyeglasses, and when we shake hands, I notice that he has the softest skin I've ever felt.

"I'm a big fan, man," Steve says, gripping my right hand in both of his velvety palms.

Once we're inside, though, I have to admit that the theater space itself is very cool. It's a thrust stage, as Anna said, with seats on three sides of the performers, and there's even a small balcony. There are more seats here than in the playhouse, but everything feels pulled in tight to the stage. It's hard to imagine any show here not feeling close and intimate. In short, it's sort of the perfect place for our music.

"All right," Steve says, "I'm going to let you get settled for a minute and then we'll give it a whirl, okay? I'm going to listen from the booth."

Anna unpacks her violin while I set up a simplified version of our recording and playback equipment.

"What's up with his hands?" I whisper to Anna, but she only gives me a bemused smile, then shrugs and starts running some warm-ups on her violin. I should be warming up my voice, too, but I'm so tired that I'm having a hard time accomplishing much of anything. Instead, I sit dumbly and listen to Anna, who sounds beautiful in here, the notes of the violin like bright splashes of paint inside the black box.

The stage lights come up slightly, and then there's Steve's voice coming out of nowhere, telling us to take it from the top whenever we're ready. I feel like I'm being sucked down a long, dark tube. We don't have all the recordings, so Anna starts us off by playing the opening theme. For a second, I am terrified that when I open my mouth, nothing will come out, but then it's there, my words echoing through the space, but somehow disconnected from me, too, as though maybe they're being boomed out from the same black nowhere that Steve's voice is coming from: "What do you do when you hear the voice of a ghost?"

I am not a total amateur. There's a sort of autopilot that kicks in; I manage to say my lines, I sing the lyrics as we've written them. I can see Anna working harder than usual to make it come together, the glisten of sweat on her forehead, the extra push that she seems to be giving the instrument. There is a part of me that wishes I could help her, that I could lift some of the weight from her. But the greater part of me is so, so tired.

We do not run the whole show. Steve breaks in at intervals, obviously working from a set of notes, asking us to do this section or that section. I hear myself talking about my brother, but I don't picture Julian as I do it, don't feel the way that Julian would wrap his arms around me when I abandoned my bed for his. We get through it, but Anna doesn't look at me when we are done.

"Everything felt off today," Anna says as Steve comes down to meet us on the stage. "We can do better than that, I promise."

"Hey, no problem," Steve says. "I get it. Adjusting to a new stage is tough. This isn't a dress rehearsal or anything." Anna looks visibly relieved, but to me these words sound empty. "When I came to the show, it was so tight that I don't have many suggestions. But I did feel like the audience couldn't get enough of your stories about Elise and Julian. I think you could expand it a little, you know? Slow down and give us even more reasons to fall in love with them."

"Sure," Anna says. "We can do that. Right?"

There's an awkward pause before I realize that they're both looking at me, waiting for my affirmation.

"Um, sure," I say. "I'll think about it."

"Great," Steve says, rubbing his soft little paws together. "Great." He says some things about a contract, about ticket sales, and for the first time, I realize that we're going to be paid to do this. This, after one of the most lackluster performances of my entire life.

In the parking garage, I tell her that I cannot drive home without getting some food and caffeine first. On the other side of the shopping complex, we find a little diner done up in a retro fifties theme, and I feel somewhat revived by the smell of french fry grease and coffee. Anna buries herself in the menu and ends up only ordering a piece of lemon pie. While we wait for our food, she wraps a straw paper around her finger over and over again.

"What exactly was going on in there?" she asks. "Are you angry at me because he happened to call me instead of you?"

"I don't know," I say, which is the most honest thing I can think of. "I couldn't feel it today for some reason." That's when I see a single teardrop detach itself from her eyelashes. She catches it with her knuckle before it can reach her cheek, but the sight of it makes me feel like there is an anvil attached to my ankle, dragging me through the vinyl seat cushion, through the linoleum floor. All the heavy topics we've talked through, all the sadness she carried about her best friend dying, the empathy she felt for me losing Julian, but it's my stupid stuff that makes her cry.

"Anna," I say, but she only shakes her head. I slide out

from my side of the booth and into hers and hug her. "It'll be okay. It was only a stutter. I'll get it back."

"Okay," she says softly, right as the waitress slides our food onto the table.

I kiss the top of her head and say, "I promise," even though she hasn't asked me to promise anything, even though I have no idea if I can deliver. We eat mostly in silence, but at least we are sitting so close that our arms brush against each other.

It's grimly dark outside, the short days making it feel much later than it is. On the way home, Anna gazes out the window, and when I ask her what she's thinking about, she says that she's trying to remember little things about Elise that we might add to the show. I try to think about Steve's suggestion as well, try to bring Julian into greater focus, but the watery memories keep slipping away from me. The only thing that is clear is the dream I had about Muriel. I keep seeing her picking those flowers, over and over and over.

I sleep a deep, dreamless sleep that night and wake feeling like a new person, as though I am literally inhabiting a new body. The terrible fuzz has been rinsed from my brain, and I feel stupid for having been dragged into such a dark place simply because I was tired. Even better, a solution to our creative problems has been delivered to me in the middle of the night. It slipped into my brain while I was unconscious and now it is there, a gift, fully formed, waiting only for me to capture it on paper.

All day, my body is in the world, going through the motions of getting dressed, driving, going to class, but my mind is elsewhere. I scribble in my notebook new lyrics, new stories. I have that great rushing waterfall in my chest, which only happens when I know something is good. When I imagine the soulful strains of Anna's violin music added to this new material, I get actual goose bumps. After school, I drive straight to her house. I know I must look like a puppy scratching at her door, eager to show her the bone that I dug up, but I can't wait another second.

"I've been writing new songs," I say as soon as she opens the door. I wait to see amazement bloom on her face, and a little of that does surface in her eyes, and yet, and yet… the joy I've been feeling all day looks more like relief on her. Never mind. She'll see.

Anna was doing homework before I arrived, and she's still in the process of shifting gears and tuning her violin, but I blurt it out anyway: "Get this. I'm going to drop the stuff about Julian for this run, and I'm writing all new material about Muriel. That way, the show becomes this living thing that's constantly changing, constantly evolving. It's a reflection of what we're thinking about in that moment. Imagine it: People will want to see it again and again, because they'll want to know what the show has become. They'll pay for tickets again and again, too, not that it's about the money. Even the title makes sense now, because there are all these ghost versions of the show stacked on top of one another."

"Muriel?" Anna says, coughing up the word like a little bone that's gotten stuck in her throat.

"But don't worry. It doesn't mean that you have to get rid of the Elise material before the Circle Tour shows. You can keep it for as long as it feels relevant to you. You can keep it for a year if you want."

Anna drops heavily onto the couch, still holding her violin. "Who's Muriel?"

I shake my head, frustrated that the conversation is getting bogged down by details. I'd been so sure, had *trusted*, that Anna would be able to see the art of what I was doing without turning it into some stupid romantic melodrama. "I introduced you to her at the playhouse, didn't I? But the new songs aren't really about her; they're about *life*."

"She's your ex, right? The one with so many issues that she was impossible to be around?" Anna says.

"I mean, that's the point, really, how her issues were probably a reflection of my own. How we were powerful mirrors, intensifying each other's worst tendencies until it was this laser beam that neither of us could control. Can't you imagine some of the cool imagery we could work in? Like maybe some giant mirrors in front of the audience that force them to confront their own reflections?"

"Liam," Anna says. "This is madness."

I lick my lips, which are suddenly very dry. "Look, I knew that the timing would make you nervous. But we can pull it together quickly. I've already written some new violin melodies that are going to highlight everything that people love most about your sound. It's going to be..." I'm still searching for the right adjective when I recognize the hard glint of anger in Anna's eyes. While she is speaking, I cannot look at her face. I look instead at Twyla, curled on the couch, trembling like the Greek oracle she is, her cataracts like tiny, mirrored discs.

"Timing?" she says. "No, Liam, this isn't about timing." She shakes her head as though she's trying to rid herself of any knowledge of what I have just told her. "I mean, for fuck's sake. We built this show together in some of the most vulnerable moments of our lives. That's what the show is about. It's not only about Julian or about Elise; it's the story of us. And I'll tell you what it's not. It's not some blank canvas that you can fill up with sad doodles about your ex-girlfriend."

I feel myself pushed under a swell of sadness. Oh no, not this. After everything, she's as ugly as everyone else. She wants to hold me back, to keep me from doing what I know I can do. What I have always been meant to do. "Wait to make a judgment. Let me show you some of the new stuff I've done," I beg.

"I don't want to hear it," Anna snaps. "I don't want to hear about Muriel. And I don't want to scrap the music we agonized over together to learn songs that you plucked out of thin air in a single day. I want you to help me perform this show, *our show*, not make everything harder."

I feel everything break apart in this moment, crushed under the pounding wave. I feel the world splinter and skitter apart into separate pathways. Why can't she see that if one world becomes many, one show has to become many, too? I close my eyes against the dizziness. The creative energy that has been animating me all day seeps from my limbs, and I wait to see which giant cosmic drain I'm about to be sucked down.

Everything goes quiet in the room then, the wave pulled out with the tide. I feel Anna put her hands on my shoulders, feel her kiss my temple the way my mother would do when I was a small child. "I'm sorry," she says. "I'm protective of what we made together, because it's so, so important to me. But I shouldn't have been so mean." She leans her forehead against mine. "The reason we have this opportunity is because they love the show we made so much. We have to deliver that same show, at least this time. You can see that, right?"

"I don't want to talk about my brother anymore," I say, my eyes still closed. This surprises me, because the whole day I haven't been thinking much about Julian, haven't been dreading speaking about him onstage, but it is nevertheless true. "I don't want him to die up there over and over again."

"I'm sorry," Anna says again. She sighs, and her face is so close that I can smell the coffee on her breath mixed with something artificially sweet, and I flinch. *I loved you ever, I loved you ever, I loved you ever.* "After this, you can write an entire show about Muriel, and I'll play violin," she says. "I'll collaborate on the music as much as you want me to. But can we please, please do our show at the Circle Tour? Can you please do it for me?"

So this is the world I am in now; this is the direction in which I am hurtling. I can see the future so clearly. I know what is coming next, even if she doesn't. What choice do I have but to follow the melody that's already begun? I open my eyes and look at Anna. Sometimes, when she's very stressed, she gets a tic in her left eyelid, and I can see it trembling there now. Twyla gives one belated yip of warning, and then settles her head back down to sleep.

"Of course," I say. "I guess we better practice."

For the next two weeks, time passes strangely, not flowing forward, but getting sucked into back currents and eddies that leave me feeling like we will always be getting ready for the performance but never actually performing it. Eventually, though, we are perched on the lip of our very own black hole: opening night.

The lobby of the Circle Tour, cramped and curved, does not lend itself to the same mingling with audience members that had been part of the show at the playhouse. Instead, Steve has asked us to stay backstage. Anna hovers near the stage entrance as the seats fill, barely keeping her toes behind the reflective tape that marks the audience sightline.

"I see our parents," she says. "And a few people from school. But it's mostly people I've never seen before." She exhales audibly, a low whistle. "I guess that's good, new people seeing the show. But it sort of makes me want to throw up, too." I'm not sure if she's talking to me or to herself. I walk up behind her and put my arms around her waist, bury my face in her hair.

"I've always loved the smell of your shampoo," I say.

"Huh," she says. "Really? It's drugstore stuff, nothing fancy."

"Anna," I say, but she's the one who says perfect things, and there's nothing to say anyway, really, so I only repeat her name, tasting it in my mouth. "Anna. Anna."

"Liam, Liam, Liam," she says, giving a nervous laugh, and then she turns around to look at me. "It's time. Ready?"

I'm not, so instead of saying yes, I say, "Let's go."

We walk onto the stage, take our seats, and begin the show. It feels so familiar, this thing that didn't even exist a few months ago, and we fall into it like putting on a comfortable jacket. But it's better than it has been these past few weeks of rehearsal; being in front of an audience has given the material its energy again. Anna has added a few anecdotes about Elise, even added one new song to please Steve. It's not bad, but I don't think it brings anything extra to the show. As for me, I told Steve that there's nothing more to say about Julian, because I'm dealing with scant memories from early childhood, and Steve, to his credit, did not push the matter further.

It's not until the last third of the show that I begin to depart from the script. There's a song about what it means to remember things, about what it's like to exist in the present moment and a past one at the same time. Anna plays the simple, pretty melody that we composed together, exactly as we've rehearsed, but I have written new lyrics in place of the final verse. "But this moment is a memory, too, one we haven't yet had time to remember. How will we look at it, how will we feel when the present has burned down to an ember?"

Anna notices the difference, of course she does. I can feel her give me a tiny sideways glance, but there's not the slightest hitch in her playing. The violin gives nothing away to the audience. When the song ends, I lean into the microphone and look at the audience, really study them for a few seconds. I can feel them getting uncomfortable quickly.

"This is where I usually talk about the ghosts of our former selves, about what it felt like to realize that Anna and I had written music together before, when we were little kids, about how we both almost forgot that, almost lost it forever. But tonight, I want to talk about something else. I want to talk about what it feels like to become a ghost of who you want to be. Right now, in this very moment." I can feel Anna go very still beside me, a rabbit that is trying to avoid the notice of a predator. "See, I like trying on different personas. I've liked coming up on a stage and performing the role of sympathetic little brother, generous boyfriend. But that can only last for so long."

I turn to look at Anna. Her face is frozen except for that tiny tic of her eye, and only I can see that. "Anna's not the villain of this story. She didn't have to talk me into any part of this. But she did allow me to see the truth when she spoke to a newspaper reporter about my band in the past tense."

Anna doesn't bother to speak into the microphone, but it picks up her voice anyway. "Liam, I didn't mean that. I apologized for—"

"When she said that, I started thinking about who I am at my core, about what parts of me don't change. What I realized is that I'm essentially a fuckup." The audience is shifty now, whispers starting to surface, the tremors of uneasiness taking hold. "I didn't fulfill my original purpose of saving Julian, and here I am, still fucking up this story that's supposed to make sense. But I'm also a rock star, and if I'm a failing one, so be it, but I do that right now, in the present moment, not in the past."

"Liam, don't," Anna says. The hand gripping her violin has tightened so much that it's white, completely bloodless.

"Anna told me recently that this is a show about us." I look out into the audience again. Most of them look confused, unsure what they're watching, unsure whether or not

Anna's confusion is part of the show. For a second, my eyes fall on my mother, who doesn't look confused at all. She looks disappointed, but not surprised, as though she was expecting to be let down all along. "She was right. It's about finding that real, true particle of yourself among all the ghost versions. And this is the most honest version of myself that I can give you. This is what it looks like when I ruin something." I mean to deliver this last line straight to Anna, but I lose my nerve at the last second and say it to the audience instead.

I turn to look at her. She isn't crying like I thought she might be, but she doesn't look like the girl from Elise's funeral, either. I have that strange feeling of vertigo again, wondering who she is, and now, despite the claims to the audience that I've just made, I wonder who I am, too. *This is what it looks like when I perform this show for the last time*, I think. *And this is what it looks like when I leave you.* I haven't done it to hurt her—I have known that from the first time the idea crossed my mind—but I wonder momentarily if this was all an elaborate way of hurting myself.

"I'm sorry," I say, and then I turn and flee the stage. I grab my coat on the way out the back door. Behind me, I can hear Anna start to play the violin, a song that is similar to what we've written but not quite the same. Whatever she does next will probably make the audience love her more than ever. She'll be all right.

Outside, I feel like an injured bird—wounded, wheeling,

but released from gravity. I run down the manicured sidewalk lining the edge of the shopping area, careening in the dark to the front of the building. There is nothing to do but run—Anna drove me down here, and I can't very well loiter around the theater until my scandalized parents emerge with the rest of the audience. But then, as though we have been timing it precisely, I round the corner in the same moment that Muriel flies out the front door of the theater and whirls around in her green coat to lock eyes with me.

"You," I say, stopping in my tracks and panting. "I didn't know you were here tonight."

"Here I am," she says, walking toward me.

"Well, sorry then, I guess," I say. "Fuck. I can't believe I actually did that."

"It was exhilarating," she says, a faint smile on her face. "Like watching someone jump out a window." I'm not sure if this is really meant to be a compliment or if she's only kidding, but I don't care right now.

"Give me a lift?" I ask. "Before the angry mob comes after me?"

"Sure," Muriel says, her smile widening. "Race you to the car."

We run to the parking garage, both of us intermittently succumbing to fits of hysterical laughter. The new and improved cross-country Muriel outpaces me easily, even in her high-heeled green shoes.

21

TO THE LEFT

THERE IS NOTHING LEFT to do but run away.

The extra keys to my dad's car are in my hand, though I don't remember looking through my bag for them. I've left my violin on the floor in the wings of the stage; I don't bother to pick up my bag or even my coat. None of those things matter in the slightest anymore. Instead, I stagger through the lobby, empty of everyone save a few latecomers, and into the parking lot, my left arm held against my body like a crumpled, misshapen wing.

My father's car is a terrible shade of green, embarrassing to borrow for any purpose, but now the color is an asset, easy to spot among the sleek gray and black and white cars that fill the rows. I collapse into the driver's seat, shivering with equal parts pain and cold, and force my injured hand to grip the steering wheel. I am disgusted with the whimpering sound that comes out of my mouth.

Time has ceased to be a smooth, uninterrupted line and is instead a series of broken shards: the confused look on the face of the parking lot attendant as I blow past him without paying, the bleat of horns as I career around a right turn without looking for oncoming traffic, the sign that marks the on-ramp of the highway, so green that it can only be destiny to steer toward it.

I was the girl who fell from the sky, the girl with a second chance too precious to waste, the girl meant to touch the clouds. I was too dumb to realize, though, that my wings melted off long ago, and I was never meant to fly after all. My arm has liquefied; it is nothing but a watery wax that will never harden again.

It's a small highway, only four lanes, barely any distance between my own trajectory and the cars that are speeding past in the opposite direction. If I turn the wheel the tiniest bit, this can all be done, I can finally feel the impact that I somehow missed all those years ago when I hit the ground. I see a truck coming toward me, attaining a speed that should be impossible for a vehicle so hulking. The headlights meet my gaze, two pairs of eyes locked in a staring contest. We recognize each other, though I'm not sure how, and a throb of déjà vu passes through my body and settles into my wrist, the seat of all pain. The truck leers at me, a ghost from the world of nightmares.

At the last possible second, my hands snap the steering wheel to the right instead, cutting across a lane, a symphony of squealing brakes and blaring horns climbing to a crescendo in my wake. I am waiting for a crash, a massive jolt, but it never comes. Instead, I careen over the shoulder and into the weeds before my reflexes take over and I slam the brakes. The car bumps along in the ditch for a stretch and then judders to a stop.

I could have killed someone, and it's hard to believe I haven't. I bury my head in my hands, barely able to hear the rising sound of the sirens behind me.

"Oh, Anna," my mother says as she runs toward where I am slumped on a bed in the emergency room. "Oh, Anna, oh, Anna, oh, Anna." She seems to have lost all her other words in the confusion.

I will learn later that my parents were utterly bewildered when the concert started without me onstage. They left their seats and tried in vain for a while to locate me but found only my abandoned instrument, setting off a small panic. They were trying to remember where they parked the car when a theater employee ran after them and said that an emergency room nurse was trying to reach them on the phone in the ticket office.

"Oh, Anna," my mother says once more, running her fingers over the bulky bundle of ice that they've bandaged to my arm. A badly damaged tendon, but not completely ruptured. It could heal with the right kind of physical therapy. A young emergency room doctor told me all this without ever fully looking me in the face.

"Where's Dad?" I manage to say, though the pain medication they gave me has turned my tongue to oatmeal.

My mother sighs, trying to relocate her ability to speak. "Trying to get the car back," she says, and then, seeing the tears roll down my cheeks, she adds, "Don't worry about that right now."

"I couldn't do it," I say, blubbering. "I was supposed to be twice as great. That's what you always said."

"I never meant…," my mother starts, and then words fail her again. "Oh, Anna," she says one more time, but she takes me in her arms, the strong, sinewy arms of a dancer, and she holds me tightly to her chest as though I am a baby. "Your mere existence is a miracle to me. You don't have to be anything more," she says, and even though I know that this isn't fully true and that she's only saying this to comfort me, my heart gives a heaving sob of its own because it's all I ever wanted to hear.

When I call Mr. Halloway to tell him that I'm sorry about leaving before the concert and that I am dropping out of the orchestra, he is gracious and kind.

"You're a very good violinist, Anna," he says. "Rest that

arm; let it heal. You're welcome back whenever you're ready."
I tell him that I will be back as soon as physically possible and
almost hang up before he adds, "It's going to be okay. Even
if you aren't able to come back at all, it will still be okay. I
mean that." I can't find the words to respond to this last statement, so I place the phone soundlessly back on the receiver as
though I never heard it at all.

I am sitting on the steps in front of the school one day, waiting
for my mom to pick me up and drive me to physical therapy,
when I feel someone gently kick my lower back. I don't turn
around; I already know it is Elise, who has been assiduously
ignoring my very existence for the better part of a month. She
sits down beside me.

"Heard you broke yourself," Elise says.

I sniff. "Who told you that?" I ask, quietly terrified that
Elise will say, "My cousin," because Liam is one topic that
would truly break me if I have to deal with it right now.

But Elise only says, "A little bird." She's quiet for a minute,
then she hooks her thumbs together and flies her hands up
like a bird to perch on my shoulder. She pecks gently at my
neck with her thumb, and I twist away and smirk to keep
from smiling. Elise drops her hands down to her lap again,
and we sit there for another minute, trying to figure out a way
toward what we know has to come next.

"Sorry," I say. "I shouldn't have interfered. It didn't have anything to do with me, really."

"That's okay," Elise says. "They would have known anyway. I was being dumb." I nod, but I wish Elise would elaborate. Was it those afternoons with Eric that she regretted? Or was it merely being careless enough that her parents caught her? "Sorry I was mean to you," Elise says.

This is always the phrase that Elise uses to apologize, the magic words she has repeated since we were children. They always signal the end of the fight. They're still applicable here, but they don't seem to carry the same power they normally do. I wrap my arms around myself to ward off the chill. I want Elise to say the perfect thing to fix everything, but she looks tired, as tired as I feel. I'm not sure that either of us can rebuild the struts and supports that have broken. Elise tilts her head back, studies the sky.

"I think it's supposed to snow tonight," she says. My mom's car turns into the lot.

"I don't think so," I say, standing up and shouldering my pack with my good arm. "It's not cold enough."

"Okay," Elise says. "But if it does snow, you have to be my friend again." I say nothing to this, but as I open the passenger side door, I hear her call out, "Deal?" and I say, "Deal," over my shoulder, loud enough to be heard.

Later, when my mom is driving us home from Movewell Physical Therapy and she turns the wipers on to combat the sloppy, wet flakes that are plopping onto the windshield, I feel tears of relief prickle against the surface of my eyeballs, almost as if they are coming from the outside like precipitation.

When Elise picks me up for the Science for Everyone lecture a few nights later, she's wearing oversized tortoiseshell eyeglasses and a tight pink sweater.

"Since when do you need glasses?" I ask.

"Nonprescription lenses," Elise says. "I'm going for a sexy librarian thing so I can pick up a scientist tonight." I roll my eyes but silently admit that Elise has really hit the mark. It had been Elise, of course, with her talent for knowing about every available social event, who saw the poster for this lecture series at the nearby branch campus of OSU.

"Probably a bunch of nerds drinking beer," she told me on the phone. "But they're doing meteorology this Thursday, so we have to go, right? Maybe then you'll actually know when it's going to snow."

It turns out that Elise has undersold the event, not a typical tendency of hers. There are a lot of people milling around outside one of the school's larger lecture rooms, buying popcorn and little plastic glasses of wine from the refreshment tables. There are some college kids here, but older people, too, and even a few teenagers other than us. Everyone is eating and drinking and enjoying one another's presence, and it isn't until the moment when the audience is making their way to their seats that I realize it feels a little like the group camaraderie of orchestra practice. Or rather, it seems like the easygoing fun that everyone aside from me always seemed to be having at orchestra practice.

The mere thought of rehearsal makes a little bubble of dread rise up in my chest. Sergei called me the day after the concert, and I still haven't returned his call. Any stray thought of Sergei or Liam is enough to make me nauseous, to say nothing of Call-Me-Gary.

Elise drives her pointy elbow into my side, interrupting my train of thought. "I'm pretty sure that meteorologist is checking you out," she whispers.

I don't bother to look at the person Elise is indicating. I don't need another crush, incoming or outgoing. I'm just relieved to have Elise back. But I do ask, "How can you tell he's a meteorologist?"

"It's kind of weird—he's carrying this weather map around his neck that he keeps pointing to," Elise says, and we both dissolve into giggles as the first speaker shushes the crowd.

The next ninety minutes are entertaining. I finally admit to myself, while a history professor is making jokes about bygone ways of predicting the weather and Elise is snorting with laughter, that I remember what having fun feels like. I watch Elise taking notes and imagine her as a meteorologist.

But then I remember that Elise changes her mind about the future multiple times a day. It makes me jealous, Elise's chameleon-like qualities, but then...maybe I could be the same. Maybe I don't have to be the person I always expected myself to be.

At the end of the presentations, we are already making plans to come to the next lecture in the series when we see Elise's mother standing in the parking lot. Her expression is impossible for me to read, but it isn't projecting good news. Had Elise, still under house arrest or something, not told her parents she was coming here? No, it's not anger on her mom's face. Elise goes still beside me, and then, better interpreting the negative vibrations in the air, sprints toward her mother. I walk quickly in their direction, but I am not close enough to hear Elise's mom's words. Whatever she says makes Elise crumple, makes her drop to the pavement and clutch her hair. Her mother squats down to rub her back awkwardly, but Elise pushes her away.

"You hated him anyway," I hear her say as I approach, and I know somehow, even if I won't hear all the details until later. The mix of drugs in his bloodstream, the lack of skid marks that indicated he blacked out or maybe had a seizure, the car wrapped around a tree—these facts I'll comb over in the days to follow, but in the parking lot, I know with perfect clarity, even before Elise's mother murmurs the news in my ear, that Eric is dead. I feel a swoop of vertigo, see the ghost truck locking eyes with me. So that was it, then. It had come for Eric instead of me.

"Can you drive the car to your house?" Elise's mom is calmly asking me. "We'll come get it tomorrow." She doesn't wait for me to answer, just slips a set of keys in my pocket and then pulls Elise's elbow until she is standing. Elise's mom seems so in control that I imagine she would simply lift Elise and slide her into the trunk if that was what was required.

"Elise," I say, and she looks at me even though her head has been buried in her hands. She waits for me to say the right thing for this singular moment. But my mind goes blank. I refuse to say any of the usual idiotic things that people say when there's a death, and I don't know how to explain that it was supposed to be me instead of Eric, so we stand there mute until Elise's mom opens the passenger door and gently pushes Elise inside.

"Thanks, Anna," Elise's mom says before she gets in and starts the engine, though I don't deserve to be thanked for anything.

I'm not technically allowed to be driving; my license was revoked for six months after my recent highway stunts, and the brace on my wrist makes steering difficult. Even so, I manage to pilot the Monopoly mobile to safety. When I switch from the cassette tape that Elise had been playing to the radio, I realize that she had it tuned to the classical station. It's strangely touching, the idea that Elise was listening to "boring music" because of me. But then, where Elise is concerned, who ever really knows what she is thinking?

I want to go to the wake to support Elise, so my dad drives me. He asks if I'm doing okay; I can hear him striving, under the words, to do the right dad thing, so I decide to let him attempt to help me. It's something I've been trying with my parents in the days after the concert, with mixed results.

"I'm all right," I say. "But I don't want to say the wrong thing. I mean, what can I possibly say that won't make everyone feel worse?"

"Yeah, that's a tough one." My dad grimaces and squints at the road, and I think for a moment that this might be all he has to say about the matter, but then he says, "When Grandma died, I think I wanted people to say they would remember her, you know? I wanted to know that she mattered to people and that I wouldn't be the only one carrying the memory of her into the future. So maybe you could say something you like about Eric."

I lean my head against the cold car window and close my eyes. I knew he would offer some piece of advice along these lines, which is fine except for the fact that I didn't really like Eric. This is the first time that I have had to grapple with the contradiction that you could not care about a person at all and still, in some primal human way, not want them erased from the world with the single surge of a car engine. Even if I didn't see Elise's terrible anguished face every time I closed my eyes today, I still wouldn't want an Eric-sized hole ripped in the fabric of the universe.

"Maybe the best thing to do is to keep it really simple," my dad says, still trying to be helpful.

"Okay," I say as I get out of the car. "Thanks. I'll find a ride home."

"Anna," he says, leaning to look at me before I shut the door. "Don't worry about saying the right thing. You're a good person, and people can feel it. That's enough." I wave at him as he pulls away, feeling a little sorry for him. It is a weakness of parents, thinking that the whole world sees you the same way they do.

I have never met Eric's mom, but I immediately identify her, because she looks exactly like Eric. I can't make myself go talk to her, can't bring myself to shuffle through that sad line of people in front of the casket, and I look around desperately for a diversion, but the room is full of strangers, clusters of kids from Eric's school. Elise is nowhere to be seen. I stand awkwardly in a corner of the room trying to think of what to do with my hands.

"Here," a voice says, and when I look over, Liam is handing me a bottle of water. "You still sort of look like a hall monitor, even at a funeral."

"Oh," I say, looking at the bottle for a moment like it's a

245

scorpion. I knew that he would be here, but in my imagining of this scene, I thought I might be so preoccupied with comforting the hysterical Elise that maybe I could avoid him altogether. I realize that I am still staring at the bottle dumbly, so I snatch it out of his hand.

"Is this better?" I say, holding the bottle stiffly in front of me. "Do I look cooler?"

"Much," he says. "It's very important to look cool under these circumstances."

I say the next part fast, before I can chicken out or think too much about it. "I'm really sad about Eric, and I'm not saying that as some bullshit polite thing I have to say. I know he was your friend, and he was Elise's friend, and even though I didn't know him very well, I really, really wish that none of this had happened."

Liam waits for a pause in my rush of words, studying me carefully. He takes a swig of his own water before saying, "Okay." He pauses and then adds, "It's cool of you to come to this."

My father's advice to keep it simple isn't going too terribly, so I take a deep breath and go on to the other thing. Might as well get it over with. "And I'm sorry about...what happened at the concert. It was totally out of line, and all I can say is that there was a lot going wrong for me right then, and I guess I kind of lost my mind for a minute."

"You already apologized," he says.

"I did?"

"Yeah, I helped you downstairs before you ran off, and you said you were sorry about a thousand times."

"I don't remember that at all."

"I think you were in a lot of pain." Liam shrugs. "I told you then and I'll tell you now that you don't need to apologize." I am unsure what to make of that shrug—as though there are women collapsing into his arms and kissing him every time he turns around—but even so, I feel a great deal of relief. "I mean, I can't say much about your taste in make-out partners since I was acting like a dick at the time." He grimaces as though he's about to intentionally drop something heavy on his own toe. "Elise is her own person, it's true, but you were only trying to be a good friend. I guess I'm saying...sorry."

"Apology accepted."

"I should have tried a little more with Eric, apparently," Liam says.

"Oh, Liam, don't. Surely you don't think that anything you could have—"

Liam waves my words away. "It's all right. We don't have to have that conversation. Of all people, it's not up to you to convince me I'm a good person. I'm sorry I got on your case for doing what you thought needed to be done. That's all."

I don't know what to say to this, so I slowly unscrew the cap on the bottle of water and take a long drink. Across the room, Elise enters with her parents. She is quiet, not at all hysterical, though her face is puffy with already cried tears. She is wearing an understated black dress, but she's also wearing a wide, flat black hat pinned at an angle. The sight of her makes me feel better somehow; even tragedy has not managed to completely flatten Elise's personality.

"Speaking of," I say, nodding toward them. "I should go keep her company. Thanks for the water." I start to walk away but stop when he says my name. Turning back toward him, I take in the whole of him for the first time today, noticing how handsome he is in his dark gray blazer.

"It was nice, when you kissed me," he says, and I feel the blood whooshing loudly and uncomfortably in my ears. The kiss comes back to me then, in a way I've been afraid to remember in the intervening weeks: the solid feel of him against me, the soft shape of his lips, the sense that the world had slowed on its axis. "And when I really stopped and thought about it, I did remember you. From when we were kids. We made that radio show together, the three of us."

I have a hard time swallowing. I want to flee so badly, but I know that my future self will never forgive me if I don't take some sort of chance in this moment. "Do you...I mean, maybe we could get away from this later. Get some ice cream or something."

He smiles at me, maybe with apology in his eyes, maybe with pity. "I have a girlfriend. On and off again, but right now...we're on again."

"Of course," I say, wanting to dissolve into a million particles tiny enough to disappear into thin air. "Well. Bye."

"I'll see you around," he says.

"You didn't have to come," Elise says to me later, when we're sitting on our favorite corner couch in Higher Grounds. She took off her dramatic hat when we walked in and placed it gravely on the head of the cashier when he gave us our orders, and without questioning it, he has left it there as he serves other customers. Elise looks small and vulnerable without it. "I know you hate stuff like that, where you have to make small talk with people."

"Of course I came," I say. "Besides, whether or not a person likes chitchat—I'm not sure funerals are a ton of fun either way."

"Maybe, though. Maybe there are people who show up there for the fun of it. Like crashing a party but with no dancing and worse food."

On the drive over here, I took a deep breath and tried to give Elise the same statement about Eric as I'd given Liam, but she had shushed me. "Oh, shut up, Anna. I know you're not a monster who wanted him dead."

I'd backed off the topic then, but it seems absurd to be talking about the upcoming winter break or reruns of *Seinfeld* when there's an elephant named Eric sitting in the coffee shop with us. I try again to tell the truth, to keep it simple: "I've been worried about you since Thursday night. How are you doing?"

"It feels like a bad dream. But, like, only a bad dream. Meaning I'm mostly okay," Elise says. "And I don't know, I kind of feel like a piece of shit because I'm okay, you know?"

"I'm not sure I follow."

"I'm supposed to wish I was there, right? If it had been only a few weeks earlier, I probably would have been. I'm supposed to wish I was there because then I could have stopped it from happening or at the very least, he wouldn't have had to be alone. And I do feel that sometimes. But there's this other part of me that really doesn't want to be dead. It's kind of like relief." She pauses for a second, looking at me, and I realize that she's searching my face for judgment. "And then the relief makes me feel even worse, and I go through the same cycle of emotions over and over again."

"That sounds exhausting," I say, because I know a thing or two about getting stuck in cycles of thinking about myself. I can feel my healing wrist pulse inside the brace with a kind of sympathy pain, and for a few seconds, I envision my disembodied arm in the passenger seat of Eric's car, speeding along toward disaster. Then I take a deep breath and calmly let go of the image, because that's another thing I've been trying.

"I guess I don't have to tell you that you couldn't have stopped this from happening. It's not like Eric was particularly interested in anyone telling him what to do."

Elise shakes her head. "You don't know that. Nobody knows that."

"Well, let me be the one who feels guilty about it," I say. "I'm *glad* you weren't hanging out with Eric when this happened. I *am* relieved, because I can't stand the thought that you might have been in that car crash. I'd never survive that. I'd never be able to go on living my life if that happened."

"That's not true," Elise says. "There's a reason for the phrase 'life goes on.'"

"No," I say stubbornly, because it is true. "The world would stop without you in it."

I have not been practicing. After the concert, I was ordered to stop practicing altogether by Polly, the unfailingly upbeat physical therapist who reminds me of my elementary school gym teacher, and instead do her awful exercises. The exercises are not only agonizing but also boring, and it is hard not to view them as punishment. I do them religiously anyway, because I am still me.

After a few weeks of this, though, Polly makes some notes on her clipboard and says, "Okay, I know you're probably dying to get that violin in your hands again. Let's talk about how to counteract the repetitive stress going forward."

"Wait," I say, "I can start playing again?"

Polly puts down her pen and looks at me with mild

surprise. "Haven't I been telling you what great progress you've been making?" This was true, but I figured affirmations were something that poured from Polly regardless of how well or horribly a patient was faring. "Girl, you're practically finished here. Just a few follow-ups to make sure that mobility keeps improving. Are you okay? Usually people can't wait to get out of this place, no matter how hard they've fallen for my charms."

I feel stupid for being gobsmacked by this news. This is why I've been coming here, after all, but I'd begun to think of the beige waiting room full of elderly people as a purgatory that I would endure forever.

"You know, I do get it," Polly is saying. "It can be scary to go back to the old routines that caused the injury in the first place."

I can't tell if that's the reason I feel so strange. It's true that I still hear music in my head all the time, but while my practice habits have been in limbo, I have stopped my usual endless thinking about the mechanics of playing—the bowings, vibrato, the exact placement of each finger on the fingerboard. Now I don't know if I can ever get that back, or if I want to.

At the end of the session, Polly gives me a hug. "You are such a champ, Anna, I mean that. Have fun playing that violin. It's going to be all right."

These are almost the exact words that Mr. Halloway said

to me over the phone. Why did adults always want to tell you that things were going to be okay when they so clearly were not?

Back at home, I sit in my room and stare at my violin case for what feels like hours. Instead of opening it, I pick up the phone and dial Sergei's number. He answers right away.

"I don't want to be anyone's girlfriend right now," I say before I can back out. "But I wish I had tried harder to be a good friend. I wish I hadn't been so caught up in my own problems whenever I was with you."

"Anna Karenina," he says. "You haven't thrown yourself in front of a train after all."

"How do you know?" I say. "Maybe I just survived it."

"If that's true, I'm glad to hear it," he says. "Orchestra rehearsal is a bore without you. When are you coming back?"

"I'm not sure I'm going to."

"I promise not to hit on you. From here on out, it will be Rachmaninoff and Karenina: The Buddy Film."

I laugh in spite of myself. "It's not that. Sergei...do you ever think about giving up the violin altogether?"

"Of course," he answers, so quickly that it surprises me. "All the time. Almost every day. Each time I have a lousy practice, I think, 'Why am I doing something so fucking hard?' But I don't know...so far it's been more interesting to keep going."

After I hang up, I get out my violin and tune it and play

a few scales, but my fingers feel big and slow, everything slightly pitchy and out of sync. I almost put it away, but then I close my eyes and play a little section of the Strauss. I'd mostly ignored this piece during my tenure in the orchestra, but now I find parts of it stuck in my head as I go through my days. I think of Call-Me-Gary saying that this piece is all about feeling: *Tod und Verklärung*, death and transfiguration. My violin has that purring resonance again, a comforting vibration that has always gone through my collarbone straight to the center of me. Just like Mr. Halloway and Polly, the instrument is trying to tell me that everything is going to be all right, and the violin, at least, seems incapable of lying.

U

In the beginning, there were only probabilities. The Universe could only come into existence if someone observed it. It does not matter that the observers turned up several billion years later. The Universe exists because we are aware that it exists.

—MARTIN REES, astrophysicist

22

TO THE RIGHT

A FEW WEEKS AFTER he ran out of the show, Muriel tells him, her head lying in his lap, that she always knew that they would get back together. They are soulmates, she insists, and always have been.

"I always thought it was more like kindred spirits," he mumbles.

"What's the difference?" she asks.

Kindred spirits, he wants to tell her, run on parallel tracks. The first time they were together, they'd been barely zippable suitcases of explosives, bombs of trauma and id, ready to blow at any moment. This time around they are more controlled, less flammable. Their twin tendencies and impulses don't make them soulmates, though. A soulmate feels different, he wants to tell her, like a harmony coming together to meet your melody. But he doesn't bother to explain, because he's pretty sure it doesn't exist anyway.

Instead, he says, "There's this thing in quantum physics. It says that there are zillions of copies of the universe, countless variations."

Muriel laughs, sits up to bite his ear. "Oh, Liam," she whispers. "You're such a weirdo."

He hasn't spoken to Anna since he ran out of the theater. He tells himself that this is for her sake, that she has no desire to look at him after what he did. But really, it's because he can't bear to see what betrayal has done to her, can't stand to see the way it has transformed the eyes he used to think he could gaze into forever.

Most people have said nothing about the scene at the theater. Maybe it was so stupid that they are scared of mentioning it. Even his mother simply glanced at him, tight-lipped, when he walked into the kitchen the next day, and then didn't speak to him for a week.

His father did mention it, though not in fury like he might have before he saw the show. Passing Liam in the hallway on his way into his office, he took off his glasses and pinched the bridge of his nose, the way he does when he has a hard day at work, and said, "Someday, Liam, maybe you'll decide to do something quietly." He hesitated before he added, "You should apologize to that girl, even if you don't want to date her."

But to Liam, what had happened with Anna wasn't dating.

It was an earthquake that had swept through his emotional life, upending everything and then subsiding.

Any illusion that he can return to his old life vanishes during the first band practice they manage to arrange in Gavin's garage.

At first it's fine: the same wood-stain smell coming from the workbench in the corner, the same half-buzzed Eric bursting in twenty minutes late, the same moody Chris noodling on his guitar instead of listening to anything anyone has to say. But when they try to warm up on some of their oldest numbers, songs he could have sung in his sleep only a couple months ago, the melody sounds brittle, the words wooden and strange. He tells himself that he is merely rusty, but an hour later, the songs sound no better, maybe even worse.

He has been planning to run past them some of the lyrics he wrote about Muriel in that burst of creativity before the rehearsals for the Circle Tour show, but now, the act seems empty, pointless. He had been able to hear so perfectly how those songs would sound set to the music of a violin. To turn them into metal songs seems wrong, a distortion rather than a transposition. Who wants to hear him sing about his ex-girlfriend, anyway? It's ancient history, he thinks, before remembering with a start that Muriel is part of his present moment.

There are other lyrics that have been buzzing at the edges of his brain for a few days that he hasn't had the heart to confront head-on. *Ice cream and sadness as the cars go by. Your grief in a cone and my failings in a cup.*

"What's up?" Gavin says, analyzing his faraway expression warily.

"Nothing," Liam says. Nothing but Anna. He won't be able to write about anyone or anything else for months to come.

23

TO THE LEFT

ELISE HAS BEEN SO subdued since Eric's funeral, so committed to staying at her house in the evenings, folding complicated origami and reading books by Camus, that Anna is surprised when she calls one afternoon to remind Anna that she's picking her up for this month's Science for Everyone lecture in a couple hours. Anna tries not to reveal how radiantly happy she is that Elise remembered.

"Do we have time to go through the drive-in at Rocky's on the way?" she asks instead. "It's the season for those peppermint milkshakes you like."

"I'll be there ten minutes early, then," Elise says, and Anna feels the bliss of life unspoiled, of certain routines that haven't yet been thrown off course. It doesn't matter that in only a little over a year, they'll be getting ready to go to college, probably in different cities, maybe different states. It doesn't even matter that Anna sort of hates peppermint milkshakes. For now, she has Elise and the entirety of the history between them.

It isn't until Anna is sitting in the auditorium, Elise slurping at a straw beside her, that she notices that the topic for the evening is quantum mechanics. The term means nothing to her. Even so, she listens transfixed as the speakers talk about wave functions and particle physics and Niels Bohr.

"Holy neutrino, Batman," Elise whispers during an applause break between speakers. "I'm totally lost."

"Yeah, I hear you," Anna says. "Let's stay for the end, though, okay?" It's true that the concepts are slippery, that Anna can't keep them straight for very long. And yet, there's something magical about a world that is all around her and completely invisible.

The final speaker puts up a slide that reads "Many-Worlds Interpretation," and a ripple of déjà vu goes through Anna, but she can't put her finger on why the words sound vaguely familiar. The professor, a jolly-looking man with an unidentifiable European accent and messy hair, is telling a story about some physicist drinking too much sherry in a bar before having the single biggest eureka moment of his life.

"Here was Everett's revelation: It was that we—all of us here in this room, for instance—are not subject to a separate set of physical laws from the quantum particles that we study. Maybe a particle is neither here nor there"—he rapidly indicates two different points in the air—"but in both places at once. And maybe the observer of that particle is also in both places at once. You see? So there is one me observing the particle in this spot and another me observing the particle in another spot. It is not one or the other, but both, and one way is not more or less likely than the other.

"But this does not happen once in our lifetimes or a few times when major changes happen. It happens all the time. It's happening now. So what do we have? A constantly expanding set of worlds, where every possible iteration unfolds. The world branches constantly, even if we—or at least these versions of ourselves—are experiencing only one branch of it."

The room explodes with excited chatter as people try to wrap their heads around the countless versions of their lives unfolding in unseen worlds. Somewhere, Anna thinks, there is a version of her whose tendon never failed her, who is still playing in the state orchestra, and who is, probably, still miserable. Anna doesn't feel miserable right now, here, in this world.

She closes her eyes and hears an entire symphony playing in exact unison until one by one, the players break off to explore their own tune, sometimes in harmony with the larger group, sometimes in dissonance, always distinct, until it is a cacophonous multitude. That is how she would score the Many-Worlds Interpretation.

When she opens her eyes, the professor is wrapping up the evening, trying to explain that Many Worlds does not erase the existence of probability: "It's important to keep track of the statistics, since even if everything conceivable happens somewhere, really freak events happen only exponentially rarely."

"Are there any constants across all of these branching worlds?" a lady in the back shouts. "Anything to tie them all together?"

About half the people begin to gather their pens and eyeglasses and scarves and empty cups and drift toward the exits, and Anna could swear that she sees Liam on the far edge of the auditorium, zipping up his coat and pulling a hat down over his ears as he slips out one of the side doors.

"That was mind-bending, that last part, but I kind of loved it," Anna says as they walk out of the building.

"I knew you would," Elise says. "Smarty-pants."

"The strange thing is that I'm almost certain I've heard about it before. A while ago. From Liam, of all people." She lingers on the memory of the kiss and can't help but briefly imagine a world in which they had decided to kiss again and again.

"Really?" Elise says. "How random."

24

THE CACOPHONOUS MULTITUDE

THEY MEET AS CHILDREN, at Elise's house, and it is as though they are connected by gravity, held always in a tight orbit around each other. After years of petitioning both sets of parents daily, Liam transfers to Anna's high school, and they become the kind of couple that everyone thinks of as a single entity. They are an emblem of togetherness for the entirety of their teenage years.

Their wedding is a small but joyful affair held in the rehearsal space of a local theater where Liam has gotten a job as the musical director. When Elise gives the toast, she admits that her personality has been shaped by the fact that she brought them together, by being a self-made third wheel for so many years. She will go on to become an internationally recognized war photographer, sending postcards to Anna and Liam's children from places they have trouble locating on a map.

They meet in middle school, at an art show featuring some of Elise's drawings, and they repel each other. Anna thinks he is rude and full of himself; Liam thinks she is uptight and boring.

They don't cross paths again until Liam is singing a solo with the state orchestra, where Anna is reigning as concertmaster. She has to stand up and shake his hand when he finishes a rehearsal, and Liam eventually recognizes her as that sour girl from his cousin's school.

"You keep rushing the ending," she tells him curtly.

That night, Liam is complaining about her to Julian, who patiently puts aside the book he is reading for his master's thesis in history. Julian is a gentle soul, always ready to help.

"Maybe the reason you're so hung up on her is because the two of you are similar," Julian says. "It sounds like she cares as much about the music as you do, which is pretty hard to do."

At the final dress rehearsal, Liam is extra careful not to rush the ending, and when he winks at Anna afterward, her face opens up for a moment.

"You sing like your life depends on it," Anna tells him that night when they are sipping soft drinks in the theater basement. It's the nicest compliment that anyone has ever paid him, and years later, when they are both famous, they will point to this moment as the one in which everything between them changed.

They meet when it feels like their daily lives have become quicksand, sucking them ever downward.

Anna stopped playing violin after the fourth or fifth time that Call-Me-Gary came onto her. The feel of the instrument in her hands had become a leaden weight instead of a comfort. She has been in and out of school, never able to settle on a major before being overwhelmed by the relentless demands of everyday life. She is back to sleeping in her old room (the one that her mother has started to redecorate two or three times before Anna moves back in and interrupts her), trying to figure out what comes next, when she decides on a whim to go out to a local bar for an open mic.

One of the acts that night is a young man with tousled hair who sings interesting lyrics in a beautiful voice and accompanies himself terribly on guitar. A blond curly-haired woman heckles him from a back booth until the bartender asks her to leave.

Anna feels so sorry for him that she goes against all her usual instincts and buys the singer a drink after he leaves the stage. "I don't know what was wrong with her," Anna says to him. "She was way out of line."

He downs half his beer before admitting that the blond is his girlfriend and that they had been fighting earlier. Anna is tipsy enough by then to tell him that he should leave his girlfriend and should also find a better guitarist. Later, they walk out to the parking lot together, hanging on to the last few minutes of the evening.

"What about me?" Anna says. "I used to be a really good violinist. I bet I could learn guitar if I tried."

And then they kiss, and it feels like the world has been remade for them, like a second chance has been laid at their feet.

They meet as the plane climbs to thirty-five thousand feet.

He almost doesn't talk to her. He's in a bad mood, having just bombed an audition in Los Angeles, but he'd already noticed a worn Ohio state orchestra sticker on her violin case when she was putting it in the overhead bin, and he can't help but ask her, right after takeoff, what town she's from. The following conversation is so easy, the hours of the cross-country flight melting away as they argue about bands and swap bad audition stories.

When he gives her his number during the descent, she smiles almost apologetically. "I'm married," she says, and his heart plummets faster than a crashing plane, and for days afterward, he is left with a feeling of bleak emptiness.

He can't know that she has tucked the little folded piece of paper with his number into her case and will leave it there, for reasons she can't explain, even to herself. Years later, when the moment is right, she will pull it out and dial and wait, breath held, for him to answer.

They meet, but not according to classical rules of time and space.

No one who works in the lab with Anna seems to understand why she stays home to pet her golden retriever, Everett, and play her violin on Friday and Saturday nights when she could be going out with the rest of them.

"Einstein was a violinist," she tells them. "He used to say, 'I see my life in music.'"

"Yeah, you're a regular Einstein," says Wilmer, rolling his eyes, but even Anna knows this is only because he is jealous of her. Everyone who works there is a little jealous of Anna, who thinks of solutions to the most vexing problems right at the moment when everyone else is ready to give up.

One afternoon, her supervisor, Julian, asks her to go out for coffee. She is anxious, thinking that he might be considering this a date, but when they sit down at the table, she sees that that's not what this is.

"I wanted to check in with you to make sure you're okay," Julian says kindly. "You seem a little isolated sometimes."

"I'm okay," she says. "But...do you ever feel like there's something missing? Like there's dark matter swirling around in your life that's supposed to have substance?" She's surprised to hear these words coming from her mouth; she hadn't intended to talk about this with anyone, least of all her boss.

"I know what you mean," he says. "I guess I always chalked it up to being an only child, but who knows? Maybe it's more than that." She will remember the look on his face when he says this, long after they go on to work at separate institutions, only running into each other at the occasional conference.

That afternoon, they make some office-centered chitchat and give each other a polite hug before going their separate ways. How strange, Anna thinks later, when she is sitting in her living room listening to a recording of *Pagliacci*. There had been some vibration between her and Julian, but it wasn't attraction, the most common sort of unspoken connection. It was something else. It felt as if she and Julian had seen the same ghost.

They meet as babies playing in the park. They meet on the school bus. They meet in the same swimming lesson where she meets Elise. They meet when one of them is the new kid in school. They meet in a college seminar about music history. They meet in a hospital on the worst day of one of their lives. They meet online and then nervously in person in the lobby of a movie theater. They meet in a café, an art gallery, a subway car.

They meet at a school concert in which both of their respective children are playing. They meet in a nursing home.

They meet.

Liam wraps up a voice lesson with a glum-looking high school sophomore who needs help with her choral audition piece. He started this gig last year to make money during college, but the truth is, he likes it. He likes drawing out a purer sound from these students who already seem so much younger than him, coaxing it out of them like carefully reeling in a fish, and he also likes seeing how universally moody they are, likes feeling a breeze of relief that high school is behind him.

Back at the apartment he shares with two other musicians, the resident trumpet player tells him there's a message on the answering machine for him. It's a long one, but he listens to the whole thing five times, until he can almost repeat it word for word.

"Hey, this message is for Liam. This is Anna, Elise's friend Anna." Here she pauses and takes a breath, which Liam recognizes as a nervous one. "I didn't realize you lived in New York, but then I saw one of your ads for voice lessons at a coffee shop I like. I'm here, too, studying physics, if you can believe it. Anyway, maybe this is weird, but I thought it'd be nice to see someone from home, and I wondered if maybe you wanted to grab a cup of coffee this weekend at the Grace Note, the place where I saw your flyer? Maybe…Saturday at three p.m.? I guess…things always felt sort of unfinished between us. I'd say sorry now, for the mistakes I made back then, but you once told me that I'd already apologized enough. All right. I'm going to hang up before I embarrass myself further. Here's my number in case you want to get in touch."

Liam finally turns off the recording and sits at the kitchen table to think. Anna, the girl who kissed him in the wings of the theater. The girl who had signaled some kind of continued interest in him at Eric's funeral, though he'd been too caught up in his own drama to find out where that could have led. He's not sure he wants to see her, though he understands it has less to do with her and more to do with remembering who he was not that long ago: so unsure of himself, so willing to see the faults in everyone around him, so quick to feel slighted and get angry.

He almost deletes the message, but then his mind sticks at her words: "unfinished business." He hears in his head a little melody: "This is a symphony that Schubert wrote and never finished." He outgrew his tendency to burn bridges a while ago, so he picks up the phone to call her back.

When Anna is in her freshman year of college at NYU and the memory of Liam dumping her onstage at the Circle Tour has become one that she doesn't chew on every single day, she gets a letter—an actual letter—with his handwriting on it. She recognizes it immediately when the dorm mailroom worker plops it down on the counter along with a package of cookies from her mother.

She wishes that the slant of the *A*s and the slope of the *N*s didn't light up the details of his face inside her brain as if someone had flipped a switch, but she can't help it. She has kept a few of the notes he wrote her while they were writing the show together, most of them simple reminders of things they'd discussed during practice, but the notes always ended with something like, "I will love you until the mountains of the world have been ground down to dust." At her most vulnerable moments, she pulls them out and rereads them, though she would never admit this to anyone.

She considers destroying the letter when she gets to her room. She could burn it in the sink, rip it into a thousand tiny pieces, fold it into a paper airplane and let it sail away from her fourth-story window. Her roommate, Joy, comes in while she's contemplating the best mode of annihilation. They are not particularly close, but in a fit of transparency, Anna explains what she's holding, and Joy says, "Fuck, Anna, don't you even want to know what it says? I want to know, and I've never met him."

Anna is not certain that there is any apology Liam could offer up that would cap the very dark, oily wellspring of betrayal that Anna can still feel burbling inside her at times. And yet, Joy has a point.

Anna,

Thanks for opening this instead of ripping it up at the sight of my handwriting. A few weeks ago, I saw you walking in Washington Square, listening to something on your headphones, and though I couldn't bring myself to approach you, I felt like the universe was insisting that I contact you. After some excessive sweet-talking of my aunt, she helped me find your address.

I've been thinking a lot since then about what an apology is supposed to be. An admission of wrongdoing? That part is easy; I was so stupid, and I'm sorry I hurt you. An explanation? That's more difficult, but I can only say that we probably met at the wrong moment, when my own demons weren't tamed enough to keep safely caged and away from you, and I've spent the past year and a half wishing that I could have kept them in check. An assertion that the same thing will never happen again? I doubt that I'll ever get a chance to prove that to you, but I do feel like a different person than I was then. That is the absolute truth, and maybe the best apology I can offer.

If it would help to hear me say any of this in person, I'd love it if you could meet me next Saturday afternoon at 3 p.m. at that little café near the West 4th stop, the Grace

Note. Just a cup of coffee, and whatever else you need. If I don't see you there, I promise I won't bother you again.

Yours, Liam

"Damn," says Joy, reading over Anna's shoulder and chewing an oatmeal cookie uncomfortably close to her ear. "So are you going to meet him or what?"

They are both nervous when they enter the café. There has been so much that has gone before, and it feels like too much to carry here, to lay out on the tiny table with the sheet music laminated to the top of it.

And yet, when they see the other's face, the first thing each feels is relief. It's like finding a drink of water when you've already resolved to finish a long, dusty hike without it—not entirely necessary for survival, but almost.

The stereo is playing the overture from Tchaikovsky's *Romeo and Juliet*, one of the most recognizable love songs of all time, but they are too involved in what the other is saying to notice. At some point, one of them places a hand on the surface of the table and the other, without pausing to think, reaches out to interlace their fingers.

Worlds turn; particles spin. The distance between them is closed.

ACKNOWLEDGMENTS

I am so grateful to the people who saw me through the completion of this book. To Ruqayyah Daud, Farrin Jacobs, and their colleagues at Hachette: Thank you for taking a chance on a book about something as unfathomable as quantum physics. Kerry Sparks, you really are a planetary force; thanks for keeping the faith.

I owe a debt of gratitude to the quantum physicists who wrestle daily with the big, slippery questions, especially Sean Carroll, Max Tegmark, and, of course, Hugh Everett. Thanks to Andrew Leahey for providing guidance on matters of music gear, vocalists, and rock and roll. Saloni Meghani, Jules Saunders Elmore, and Jason Leahey were my earliest readers, and I clung to their advice like a proton binds to a nucleus.

A million belated thanks to my numerous music teachers and my one and only physics teacher: Ettore Chiudioni,

Randy Heidelbaugh, Ann Mohr, Doug Collins, and Tom Smith. They definitely didn't pay you enough to deal with us.

To Nancy and Dwight Dunlap: Thank you for offering me the world and for enduring all those school concerts for all those years.

One of the beautiful perks of writing this book was spending time thinking of all the people who made music with me in my youth. Many thanks to my school orchestra, youth symphony, and jazz band groupie friends, including, but not limited to, Llalan Fowler, Rachel Barnette Gulas, Mignon Miller Dwyer, Steve Kennedy, Tricia Delnay, John Boyd, Dave Humeston, Jay Goyal, Tom Hankinson, Steve Yoost, Seth Roberts, and Joel Smith. This story is for you. B Period Lunch 4-Eva.

And finally, for Jason, Nora, and Winter: this world, every world, always.

SHANNON DUNLAP

is a graduate of the MFA program at New York University. Previously, she was a weekly columnist for the *Phnom Penh Post* and her work appears in the anthology *How Does One Dress to Buy Dragonfruit? True Stories of Expat Women in Asia*. She is also the author of *Izzy + Tristan*. She currently lives in Brooklyn with her husband and children.